Enjoy all of these American Girl Mysteries®:

THE SILENT STRANGER
A *Kaya* Mystery

PERIL AT KING'S CREEK
A *Felicity* Mystery

SECRETS IN THE HILLS
A *Josefina* Mystery

SHADOWS ON SOCIETY HILL
An *Addy* Mystery

THE CURSE OF RAVENSCOURT
A *Samantha* Mystery

THE STOLEN SAPPHIRE
A *Samantha* Mystery

DANGER AT THE ZOO
A *Kit* Mystery

MIDNIGHT IN LONESOME HOLLOW
A *Kit* Mystery

A SPY ON THE HOME FRONT
A *Molly* Mystery

THE LIGHT IN THE CELLAR
A *Molly* Mystery

— A *Molly* MYSTERY —

THE LIGHT
IN THE CELLAR

by Sarah Masters Buckey

★ American Girl®

Published by Pleasant Company Publications
Copyright © 2007 by American Girl, LLC

Questions or comments? Call 1-800-845-0005, visit our Web site
at **americangirl.com**, or write to Customer Service, American Girl,
8400 Fairway Place, Middleton, WI 53562-0497.

Printed in China
07 08 09 10 11 12 LEO 12 11 10 9 8 7 6 5 4 3 2 1

All American Girl marks, American Girl Mysteries®,
Molly®, Molly McIntire®, Emily™, and Emily Bennett™ are trademarks
of American Girl, LLC.

PICTURE CREDITS
The following individuals and organizations have generously
given permission to reprint illustrations contained in "Looking Back":
pp. 158–159—poster, Office of War Information, Minnesota Historical Society;
photo, Library of Congress; pp. 160–161—butcher shop, Minnesota Historical
Society; grocery items, courtesy of Strawbery Banke; grocer with customer,
Minnesota Historical Society; ration stamps, family of William R. Wood;
World War II token and ration book holder with War Ration Book One Series,
photo by John Gilman from *Home Front America: Popular Culture of the World
War II Era* by Robert Heide and John Gilman, published by Chronicle Books;
pp. 162–163—sugar stamp poster, from *V for Victory: America's Home Front
During World War II* by Stan Cohen, used with permission; rationed meat,
Getty Images; Home Front Pledge poster, courtesy Northwestern University
Library; Victory garden, *Chicago Sun Times*; pp. 164–165—Red Cross canteen,
Library of Congress; Junior Red Cross, Library of Congress; plane-spotter
materials, from *V for Victory: America's Home Front During World War II*
by Stan Cohen, used with permission; scrap metal collectors, *Minneapolis
Star Tribune*, Minnesota Historical Society.

Illustrations by Jean-Paul Tibbles

Cataloging-in-Publication Data
available from the Library of Congress.

For Jessica

TABLE OF CONTENTS

1

A DANGEROUS RIDE

Molly McIntire whistled softly as she looked across Lincoln Park. "Uh-oh!" she said.

It was a brisk spring afternoon, and the park was full of kids playing tag on the fields, swinging on the wooden swings, and flying kites in the April breeze. At the far end of the park, boys were pitching and catching balls on the baseball diamond.

Shading her eyes with one hand, Molly watched the boys for a moment. Then she began to walk her bike quickly along the edge of the park. Linda, Susan, and Emily had to hurry to keep up with her.

"What's the matter?" asked Linda.

Molly pointed to the baseball field. "My brother Ricky's over there," she said. Then she turned to Susan. "And your brother David's with him."

Susan made a face. Emily's pale cheeks turned pink with embarrassment. "I rather hope they don't see us," she said in her clipped British accent.

"How can they miss us?" asked Linda, who was always practical. "There are four of us and we're all walking our bicycles. And we have Bennett and Yank, too," she added, gesturing toward Molly's and Emily's puppies, who were running alongside the girls. "We're like a parade!"

"You won't tell Ricky why we're here, will you?" Emily asked the other girls anxiously. "He'll tease me if he knows I've forgotten how to ride a bicycle."

"We won't say a word," Molly promised.

Molly knew that Emily was an only child and she wasn't used to being teased by an older brother. Until recently Emily had lived with her parents in London. But London was being bombed by the Germans, and it was very dangerous. So Emily's parents had sent her by ship to the United States, to live with her Aunt Primrose in Jefferson.

By the time Emily had arrived, however, her aunt was in the hospital, sick with pneumonia. Molly's mother had invited Emily to stay with their family while her aunt recovered. For the last few weeks, the two girls had shared Molly's bedroom and gone to school together. They were even given their puppies, Bennett and Yank, on the same day. Molly had come to think of Emily as almost part of the family. Unfortunately, Ricky felt the same way. He teased Emily just like he teased Molly.

"Let's walk as fast as we can," Molly suggested to her friends. "Maybe Ricky'll be too busy to notice us."

The girls had almost made it past the baseball diamond when Ricky happened to look up. He was holding a ball in his worn leather mitt, and he frowned when he saw the battered red bike that Molly was pushing.

"Hey! What are you doing with my old

3

bike?" he yelled across the baseball diamond.

"Mom said I could use it," Molly yelled back, pushing the bike even faster. "Emily's using mine."

"C'mon, Ricky! Throw the ball!" David called from home plate.

Ricky scowled at his sister. "You'd better not wreck that bike," he hollered. Then he turned and pitched the baseball.

Molly and Emily looked at each other, and then they both smiled. Ricky had been so worried about his old bike that he hadn't even asked why the girls were walking the bikes instead of riding them.

After they passed the baseball field, the girls turned right onto Overlook Hill Road. Pine trees edged the winding road and gave off a sweet smell that reminded Molly of Christmas. As they climbed the hill, the girls passed several impressive houses set far back from the road. The houses had names like "Pine Forest" and "Ridgeley Park."

"This reminds me a bit of England," said

A Dangerous Ride

Emily as they walked past the estates.

Linda raised her eyebrows. "England must be pretty fancy," she said. "Some of the richest people in Jefferson live up here."

"Don't you think this is high enough?" asked Susan, resting her bike for a moment.

The girls had climbed about halfway up the hill to a fairly level area. Molly could hear the shouts of the boys playing in the baseball field below, but they sounded far away. A straight stretch of road ran gently downhill from this spot, and it felt quiet, almost deserted.

"This should be fine," said Emily, handing Yank's leash to Molly. "I'm sure I won't have any trouble if I ride downhill."

Emily had tried riding on the flat streets in Molly's neighborhood, but she had kept wobbling and falling before she could pick up speed. She'd been convinced that if she could just get off to a faster start, she'd be able to keep her balance. So Molly and her friends had brought her to Overlook Hill Road, one of the few hills in Jefferson.

Now Susan looked down the road and frowned. "Are you sure you want to try this?" she asked.

"Oh, yes," said Emily. "Quite sure." She pointed her bicycle downhill. Then she took a deep breath, swung her leg over the center bar, and pushed off.

"Pedal!" Molly called out encouragingly.

"Steer!" Linda shouted.

"And don't forget to—" began Susan.

But Emily was already skidding. With a thud, she fell sideways onto the dirt road. She slowly got to her feet and picked up the bicycle. "I just need a bit more practice," she said.

Emily tried twice more, but as far as Molly could tell, she didn't make any progress. "Didn't she say that she used to ride a bike in London?" Linda whispered as Emily stopped abruptly again, nearly tumbling over.

"That was a long time ago," Molly explained. "She hasn't been on a bike since the war started."

"My grandpa told me that once you learn

how to ride a bike, you never really forget," said Susan.

"Too bad nobody's told Emily that," said Linda. She turned to Molly. "If she doesn't learn to ride by tomorrow, you two can't be magazine girls."

"I know," said Molly, staring down at the dirt road.

"Too bad the JFA's already full," added Susan.

"Yeah," agreed Molly. She kicked a stone with her foot. *What if I don't get to do any job at all?* she worried.

At school, Molly's teacher had posted a list of volunteer jobs for kids who wanted to help with the war effort. All the kids in the class had raced to sign up. Linda, Susan, and most of the other girls had volunteered for the JFA, Jefferson's Junior First Aid program. They had already started wrapping bandages for soldiers and learning first-aid skills. They even had shiny JFA whistles, so they could call for help in an emergency.

Molly had wanted to sign up for the JFA, too. She could just imagine writing her dad, who was a doctor in the Army, about all the first-aid skills she was learning. But Emily had wanted to be a magazine delivery girl at Oak Knoll, the convalescent hospital where her aunt was a patient.

"If I deliver magazines there, I'll get to visit Auntie Prim more often," Emily had argued. *Who'd want to visit someone named "Auntie Prim"?* Molly wondered. But Emily had made up her mind, and Molly couldn't talk her out of it.

Unfortunately, Emily was the only one in the class who signed up to help at Oak Knoll. All the other kids thought that taking old magazines to a convalescent hospital sounded about as exciting as weeding a Victory garden. *I can't let Emily go all by herself,* Molly had decided. So, reluctantly, she had signed her name next to Emily's.

Molly and Emily were scheduled to begin their job after school tomorrow. They were supposed to bike to Jefferson's Red Cross head-quarters, pick up the used magazines, and then take them to the patients at Oak Knoll.

She'll never be able to bike that far, Molly thought as she watched Emily screech to a halt and almost tumble over again. *I wish we could still sign up for JFA.*

Emily turned around and marched the bicycle back up the hill. Her knees and elbows were covered with dirt, and her gingery-red hair, which was usually so neatly combed, stuck out at odd angles. "Let's go farther up," she called to the other girls. "The road might be better up there."

Linda rolled her eyes, and Susan looked doubtful. Molly shrugged. "It's worth a try," she told the other girls quietly.

The puppies eagerly pulled at their leashes as Molly, Linda, and Susan followed Emily up the hill. As she and her friends climbed higher, the road narrowed, and Molly could no longer hear the voices of the boys playing baseball.

Susan began to look worried. "We're getting close to that house," she told Molly and Linda in a low voice. "The one that everybody talks about."

Molly and Linda exchanged a glance. All the kids in town knew about Greystone Manor, the old mansion at the top of the hill.

"I've heard stories about strange noises up there at night," continued Susan. She dropped her voice to a whisper. "And some kids say that they've seen ghosts."

"Those are just stories," said Molly, trying to sound matter-of-fact. "Besides," she added hopefully, "it's still light out."

"But it's *getting* dark," said Linda, glancing up at the sun setting in the orange-red sky. She called to Emily, "Let's stop here!"

Emily was just ahead of the other girls. She turned and looked down the straight, slightly sloping stretch of road behind them. "All right," she agreed, tucking her hair behind her ears. "This should do well enough."

Molly, Linda, and Susan stepped to the side

of the road as Emily swung herself onto her bike and took off down the hill.

Maybe this time it'll work, thought Molly, crossing her fingers as the bike began to pick up speed. Then Emily wobbled and fell over, barely missing a pine tree.

"She's just scared," Linda told Molly and Susan as Emily climbed up the hill again. "She's stopping herself before she gets her balance."

Emily suddenly looked up, and her cheeks were bright pink. With a lurch in her stomach, Molly knew that Emily had overheard Linda's remark.

When Emily reached them, Susan suggested, "Maybe we should go home. It's getting late, and besides, it's dangerous to ride here."

"We can't go—not yet," said Emily, pointing her bike downhill again. "I said I was going to learn how to ride today, and I will." Emily squared her thin shoulders and then jumped on the bike and started pedaling hard.

"Oh, my gosh!" exclaimed Molly as the

bike headed down the hill, going faster and faster. Then Emily disappeared around a bend in the road. Molly dropped the puppies' leashes and chased after the speeding bicycle. Linda and Susan followed close behind.

They found Emily just around the bend in the road. She was lying in a ditch with the bicycle beside her. "Are you okay?" Molly asked breathlessly.

"Yes!" Emily announced. She looked up at the other girls, her face streaked with dirt. "I did it! I pedaled and I steered."

"Yeah, but you need to learn how to brake!" Linda told her. "That was dumb."

"You could've been killed!" exclaimed Susan. Then she gasped. "Look at your leg!"

Molly leaned forward. She saw blood trickling from a long gash down the side of Emily's right leg. Linda grabbed a clean handkerchief from her pocket. "We're learning how to bandage wounds in JFA," she assured Emily.

Susan pulled out her shiny JFA whistle.

"Think we should signal for help?" she asked hopefully.

"No one would hear you from up here," said Molly.

"Our instructor says that if you blow really hard, this whistle can be heard far away," said Susan. "It's a good way to get help."

"Thank you, but I don't really think I need help," said Emily. She stood up. "Look, the bleeding is stopping already."

"Oh, all right," said Linda, stuffing her handkerchief into her pocket.

"Do you think you'll be able to ride home?" Molly asked Emily.

"I think so," Emily said shakily. "But I'll wait till we get to the bottom of the hill." She picked up her bike. "Shall we go home now?"

Together, the girls headed back up the hill to get the other bicycles and the puppies. They found the bikes just where they had left them, but the puppies had disappeared. "Bennett!" Molly called. "Yank!"

There was no answer. All four girls started

calling. Then Emily said, "I think I hear Yank barking. Up there!"

Molly didn't stop to ask how Emily could tell Yank's bark from Bennett's. She hurried up the road. It turned sharply, then suddenly ended. A sign, hanging at an odd angle, pointed to a driveway that led downhill on the left. The old-fashioned letters on the sign read "Greystone Manor," and beneath, in smaller letters, "Currier."

"We can't go down there!" Susan exclaimed.

"Why not?" asked Emily.

Susan hesitated. She eyed the woods as if someone might be lurking behind a tree, listening to her every word. Then, in a low voice, she told Emily, "Greystone Manor has been empty for a really long time. Kids used to go there on a dare, but now…" Her voice trailed off.

"Nobody goes there anymore," said Linda, finishing the sentence for her. "Not even on a double dare."

Just then, the girls heard more barking. It was coming from the direction of Greystone Manor. "The puppies can't be too far away," said Molly. She and Emily started down the gravel driveway.

"Don't go near the house!" warned Susan as she and Linda trailed behind.

Rounding a bend in the driveway, the girls looked down at Greystone Manor. The mansion, built of slate-gray stone, rested in a bowl-like depression at the top of the hill. Tall trees surrounded the house. As the sun was setting, the trees cast long shadows, making the gray mansion look as dark and forbidding as an abandoned castle.

Molly watched the shadows of the trees dance across the cold-looking stone, and she felt a chill go up her back. She took a deep breath, cupped her hands around her mouth, and yelled, "Bennett!"

At the top of her voice, Emily called, "Yank!"

"Not so loud!" Linda told her.

"You're not scared, are you?" asked Emily.

Her blue eyes held a glint of mischief. "You said nobody comes here anymore."

"Wait a minute," Molly whispered. "Somebody *must* be here." She pointed toward the house. "Look in the cellar—there's a light."

The girls peered down at the mansion. A faint light shone in one of the small cellar windows, like an ember glowing in a pile of gray ashes.

"We can't go any closer," said Susan in a hushed voice.

"What if the puppies don't hear us calling?" insisted Emily.

Molly thought for a moment, and then she turned to Susan. "Can I borrow your whistle?"

Susan looked surprised, but she pulled the lanyard over her head and handed her JFA whistle to Molly. Molly blew two loud blasts. The shrill notes echoed through the woods. Then the girls heard more barking. The sound grew closer.

"Come on, Bennett!" Molly urged.

"Here, Yank!" Emily cried.

The puppies emerged from the undergrowth and ran up the driveway with their tails wagging furiously. Molly grabbed Bennett's leash and then picked him up, burying her head in his wet-smelling fur. "I thought you were lost!" she told him.

"Let's get out of here," said Susan. She started up the driveway, and the other girls followed.

When they reached the top of the drive, Molly glanced back at Greystone Manor. Then she stopped and stared. "Look!" she called to the others. "The light's gone out!"

"Maybe it was just a reflection of the sun," suggested Linda, walking quickly.

I'm sure it was a light, thought Molly, looking back once more at the shadowy house. *I wonder who turned it off?*

2
MISSING

The sun was shining warmly the next afternoon as Molly and Emily biked together to Jefferson's Red Cross headquarters.

"Hang on a minute!" Emily called several times as Molly got ahead of her, but she didn't fall once.

I guess the practice paid off, Molly thought.

As the girls parked their bikes in front of the Red Cross building, Molly was surprised to see her mother drive up in the family's LaSalle sedan. Mrs. McIntire worked long hours as a volunteer for the Red Cross, but because of wartime gas rationing, she usually came to work with her car pool.

Mrs. McIntire stepped out of the car in her crisp volunteer uniform. "Hello, girls," she greeted them. "Are you headed to Oak Knoll this afternoon?"

Molly told her that they were. "Why did you drive the car, Mom?" she asked.

"I had to get some things at Bartle's Grocery Store," Mrs. McIntire said. She opened the trunk of the LaSalle, and Molly saw four large brown cartons inside. Her mother picked up two of them.

"Would you like us to help you carry those?" offered Emily, who was always polite.

"Thank you, I could use some help," said Mrs. McIntire. "I need to take this oatmeal to the storeroom."

Molly and Emily each picked up a carton. Then they followed Mrs. McIntire inside the busy headquarters and down a short flight of stairs. As they walked, Mrs. McIntire said that oatmeal cookies were a favorite with the troops. "Now we'll be able to make plenty of them for the Glennings Canteen on Saturday," she said, smiling.

Emily looked puzzled, and Molly explained that Glennings was a nearby town with a busy railroad station. The Red Cross had set up the Glennings Canteen to welcome the trains full of soldiers who passed through the station. Sometimes thousands of soldiers came through the station on a single day. Canteen volunteers greeted the traveling troops and offered them free coffee, doughnuts, sandwiches, and other snacks.

"Different towns take turns bringing food, and each town likes to do something special for the soldiers," Molly told Emily. "Jefferson always makes cookies. Right, Mom?"

"Yes, it's become an important tradition," said Mrs. McIntire as she unlocked the door to the storeroom. "Our volunteer bakers make hundreds of dozens of cookies. It's our way of thanking the soldiers who are sacrificing so much for us."

Mrs. McIntire opened the door, and they carried the cartons into the storeroom. It was a small, windowless room lit by a single bulb hanging from the ceiling. Boxes were stacked on the floor, and shelves along three walls were filled with neatly organized cans, sacks, and jars of supplies.

"Let's put the oatmeal back there," said Mrs. McIntire, motioning to the far corner of the storeroom. "On the shelf below the sugar."

Molly looked around the back of the dimly lit storeroom. "Where's the sugar?"

Her mother stepped toward the shelves. "Here," she said confidently. Then she paused and added, "Well, it *should* have been right here."

Mrs. McIntire knelt down and reached into the deep shelves. She pulled a large sack of sugar from the back. "That's strange!" she exclaimed. "Just last week, we had eight ten-pound sacks of sugar here. I counted them myself to be sure we'd have plenty for the canteen. Now there's only one left."

"Maybe someone moved the others?" Molly suggested as she and Emily put the oatmeal cartons on the lower shelf.

"Perhaps," Mrs. McIntire said doubtfully. "But I don't know who would have done that. We always store the sugar in the same place." She bit her lip. "I was counting on that sugar for all our baking for the canteen. I don't know where it could be."

Molly and Emily looked at each other. Both girls knew that, because of the war, the government was rationing foods like sugar, butter, beef, and oil, as well as supplies like gasoline and rubber and other items needed for the military. "Do with less," urged posters that showed a smiling soldier, "so *they'll* have enough."

Everyone had a ration book, with stamps for buying measured amounts of rationed items. When families wanted to buy rationed foods, like hamburger or sugar, they had to give the grocer ration stamps along with their money. Because ration stamps were limited, families often had to do without meat for dinner—or sweets for dessert.

I hope Mom can find the sugar, Molly thought, looking at the storeroom's nearly empty shelf.

Otherwise, how will she get more before Saturday?

"The sugar *must* have been misplaced somehow," said Mrs. McIntire almost to herself as she looked through the shelves. Then she turned to Molly and Emily. "Thanks for your help. You'd better go get your magazines from Mrs. Fitzgerald. Good luck at Oak Knoll, and please say hello to your aunt for me, Emily."

Molly had been to the headquarters many times before, and she led Emily back up the stairs to the main desk. There Mrs. Fitzgerald, a serious-looking woman with red hair pulled into a bun, was answering questions and assigning volunteers to their work areas.

The headquarters was bustling with activity, and Molly and Emily had to wait their turn to talk with Mrs. Fitzgerald. As they stood in line, Molly kept thinking about the sugar missing from the storeroom. "Isn't it funny that so much sugar could have disappeared?" she asked Emily in a low voice.

"Funny?" Emily frowned. "No, I don't think it's funny. I think your mum's upset about it."

"I don't mean funny 'ha, ha,'" Molly explained. "I mean that it's strange. That's an awful lot of sugar to be missing. I wonder if someone stole it."

Emily's eyes widened. "That would be a terrible thing to do!"

"Do you think it's possible?" asked Molly.

"Well," said Emily slowly, "in London, I heard about people who were arrested for stealing rationed foods and selling them on the black market. My teacher said that committing a crime like that during wartime was like helping Hitler."

"There's a black market in America, too," Molly said. "When I first heard about it, I thought it was a grocery store that was painted black. Then my mom told me that 'black market' meant buying and selling things illegally. She said it could happen anywhere, but mostly it's in big cities."

"Jefferson's *not* a big city," said Emily, who had been born and raised in London.

"I know," Molly agreed. She glanced

around the crowded Red Cross headquarters. Many of the faces were familiar, and she knew that all the volunteers were working hard to help America win the war. *Nobody here would steal sugar for the black market,* she told herself. *That would be like helping Hitler!*

As she and Emily continued to wait in line, Molly looked at the notices on the Red Cross bulletin board. Someone had posted a quote from one of President Franklin Roosevelt's radio talks. Molly swallowed hard as she read it:

    All of us here at home are being
    tested--for our fortitude, for our
    selfless devotion to our country
    and to our cause.
    This is the toughest war of
    all time. We need not leave it to
    historians of the future to answer
    the question whether we are tough
    enough to meet this unprecedented
    challenge. We can give that answer
    now. The answer is "Yes."

Yes! Molly thought, staring at the typed page. *I'll be tough, and I'll work as hard as I can to win the war and—*

A voice interrupted her thoughts. "What are you doing here?"

Molly turned and saw her older sister, Jill, standing a few feet behind her. Jill was with her best friend, Dolores, and they were both wearing freshly starched pinafores. Since Jill and Dolores were in high school, they were allowed to be junior hospital volunteers. They had recently been assigned to help wounded soldiers at Jefferson's Veterans Hospital.

"We're here to volunteer, just like you," Molly said proudly.

"We're going to be magazine delivery girls at Oak Knoll Hospital," Emily added.

"Magazine delivery girls!" Dolores giggled. "Oh, that's so cute!"

Molly felt her face turn bright red. *Even Dolores thinks it's a silly job,* she thought. *I wish we'd signed up for JFA instead!*

Dolores turned to Jill. "We'd better go,"

she said, suddenly serious. "Our ride to the
hospital will be picking us up soon."

As Molly watched her sister and Dolores
hurry out of the Red Cross headquarters,
Mrs. Fitzgerald called out, "Next!"

Molly and Emily stepped up to the desk
and explained that they were supposed to
deliver magazines to Oak Knoll. Mrs. Fitzgerald reached under her desk and pulled
up two stacks of used magazines, each tied
tightly with twine.

"Here you are," she said. "When you get
to the hospital, ask for Mr. Pritchard. He's
the director and he'll tell you what to do.
And don't forget to bring any leftover magazines back with you. We can use them for
the paper drive."

Molly and Emily carried the magazines outside and put them into their bike baskets. With
Molly leading the way, the girls began pedaling
toward Oak Knoll Hospital. As they rode along
the tree-lined sidewalk, they passed patriotic
posters tacked up outside the Jefferson Town

Hall. "Keep 'em Fighting," one colorful poster urged, encouraging factory workers to produce more supplies for the military. Another poster gave Molly goosebumps. It showed Frenchmen captured by the Nazis and its caption read: "We French workers warn you: defeat means slavery, starvation, death."

The final poster showed a blonde woman in an apron. She was making the Home Front Pledge: "I pay no more than top legal prices. I accept no rationed goods without giving up ration stamps." The woman reminded Molly of her mother, and she thought again about the missing sugar.

I wonder if the sugar really was stolen, Molly worried. *But would anyone in Jefferson really take supplies that we need for the soldiers?*

It was such a terrible thought that, even though the warm sun was beating down, Molly suddenly felt cold. She knew that America could only win the war if everyone worked together. Cheating the ration system and stealing supplies was like giving aid to the enemy.

MISSING

If someone is stealing from the Red Cross, I'll do everything I can to stop it, Molly decided. *No matter what!*

Without thinking, Molly started pedaling fast, her long brown pigtails flying out behind her as she rode. She only slowed down when she heard Emily call out, "Hang on a minute!"

3

A STRANGE WELCOME

It took Molly and Emily about twenty minutes to reach Oak Knoll Hospital. The girls left
their bikes at the edge of the hospital's carefully
landscaped gardens. Then they picked up their
magazines and headed down the front path to
the main entrance.

As soon as Molly walked into the hospital,
she was struck by the smell of bleach. A thin
woman wearing a light gray dress and a white
apron was vigorously mopping the lobby.

"Excuse me," said Molly. "Could you please
tell us how to find..." She hesitated, trying to
remember the name of the hospital director.

"Mr. Pritchard," Emily supplied.

"Ah, yes," said the woman, glancing up.
There were shadows under her large brown

eyes. "Go past two doors," she said in an accent that sounded foreign. "His office is on the right."

Molly and Emily walked into the spacious central hallway. Straight ahead, there was a wide stairway leading upstairs. To the left of the stairs was a sitting area with clusters of chairs and tables. To the right was a long line of office doors.

All the walls were sparkling white, and the floors gleamed. The sound of the girls' footsteps echoed on the linoleum floors as they made their way down the hallway to the third door on the right.

A tall, spare man with thick black eyebrows opened the door before they could even knock. "I'm Mr. Pritchard," he announced in a deep voice. "You must be the girls sent to deliver magazines."

Mr. Pritchard said the word "magazines" as if it were some sort of terrible disease. Molly and Emily admitted that they were the magazine delivery girls.

The hospital director frowned. "I saw your bicycles in front of the building. Please don't leave them there again. You may put them in the back, by the delivery entrance." He looked down at their school shoes and shook his head disapprovingly. "And remember to wipe your feet before entering the building."

Oh no, Molly thought. *We haven't even started yet, and already he's mad at us.*

"The first few weeks will be a trial to see how well these magazine deliveries work," the hospital director continued. "Please remember that Oak Knoll is a convalescent hospital. Our patients are here to rest and recover. Do not talk loudly, do not disturb sleeping patients, and"—Mr. Pritchard paused, and then went on with special emphasis— "do *not* get in the way of the staff."

Molly stared at the floor. *It seems like he doesn't even want us here.*

When Mr. Pritchard finished his lecture, Emily told him that her aunt was a patient in Room 303. "May I visit her?" Emily asked.

A Strange Welcome

"Very well, young lady," Mr. Pritchard said, as if he were being particularly generous. "You may take your magazines to the third floor." He motioned to Molly. "You may take magazines to the second-floor patients. And remember, no talking! No loud noises!"

No fun! thought Molly, wishing more than ever that she had signed up for the JFA.

Molly and Emily climbed the carpeted staircase to the second floor together, and then Emily continued on to the third floor. Left by herself in the small waiting area by the top of the stairs, Molly looked at the long row of doors that opened on either side of the hallway.

I wish Mr. Pritchard would let Emily and me deliver magazines together, Molly thought. She straightened her pile of magazines, took a deep breath, and walked up to the nearest door. It was numbered 201.

A nurse with bleached blonde hair came out of the room. "Can I help you?" she asked sternly.

"I'm here to bring magazines to the patients," Molly said, trying to sound as if this were something that she did every day.

"Well, Mrs. Currier is the only patient in here, and she's asleep right now. Why don't you try another room?"

With the nurse still watching her, Molly quickly knocked on Room 202. She was relieved to find that both the older ladies in this room were awake, and they were eager to select magazines. "Thank you, my dear," said one, choosing a copy of last month's *Saturday Evening Post*. "I haven't had anything new to read in ages."

That wasn't so bad, Molly thought as she made her way to the next room. There she found two elderly gentlemen. One was snoring softly, but the other was pleased to get a copy of *Time*. His name was Mr. Emory. He looked very frail, but he insisted on showing Molly pictures of his three children. "All of them are serving in the Navy," he said proudly. "One son's a captain, the other's a lieutenant, and my daughter's a nurse in the Pacific."

Most of the patients in the other rooms were

elderly, too. But when Molly opened the door to Room 214, she found a boy who looked only slightly older than her little brother, Brad. The boy was lying in bed, encased in a white plaster cast that started at his neck and covered the rest of his body. He could only turn his head slightly when Molly came into the room.

"Who are you?" he demanded.

Molly explained her errand and asked if he wanted a magazine. "I can't hold one, can I?" he snapped. His sharp gray eyes flitted to the cast, which held his arms rigidly in place.

"Oh, sorry," said Molly. She turned to leave, but the boy called her back.

"Wait!" he ordered. "Do you have a *National Geographic*? My mother could read it to me. She comes to visit me at night, after she finishes work."

Molly showed him her small remaining supply of magazines. "All I have left are *Good Housekeeping, Ladies' Home Journal,* and *Life.*"

"I'll take a *Life,*" he grunted. "But can you bring me a *National Geographic* next time?"

He lowered his voice slightly. "I'm training to be a spy and I need to find out all I can about geography."

The boy looked so serious that Molly tried hard not to smile. "All right," she agreed, putting the *Life* on his bedside table. "I'll try to bring a *National Geographic* next time."

After Molly finished visiting the rooms, she settled into an armchair in the second-floor sitting area. Emily had said that Aunt Primrose loved to chat, so Molly guessed she would have to wait a while. She began to flip through her only remaining magazine, a frayed copy of *Ladies' Home Journal.*

The hospital floor was so quiet that Molly could hear the nurse urging a patient in a nearby room, "Take your medicine now." When the nurse came out of the room, she was pushing a cart of medications. The bottles jangled as she walked down the hall.

A big man wearing a "Laurence Laundry" uniform came out of a door at the far end of the hall. He was whistling cheerfully and he greeted the nurse in a booming voice. "Hey, Edith! I just picked up all the laundry. And I wanted to tell you that I got a letter from Pete."

"How is he?" the nurse asked eagerly. "Still flying bombers?"

"He couldn't say, but I bet he is." The man sighed and put down the laundry bag he'd been carrying over his shoulder. "I sure wish I could be there with him, but the Army says my hearing's not good enough. And they told my brother Leo that his eyes are bad. We're trying to do our part, though. Next week, we're hosting a War Bonds party. Everyone will pitch in and buy some bonds together. So if you're interested—"

"Nurse Schroeder!" Mr. Pritchard's voice sounded from the stairwell. Molly turned and saw the director standing only a few feet away. "Please remember that this is a hospital," he said, scowling. "Not a social center!"

As Mr. Pritchard continued up to the third floor, the nurse quickly wheeled her cart into another patient's room. The laundry man shouldered his bag and walked down the staircase in silence. *It looks like Mr. Pritchard won't let anyone talk around here,* Molly thought. *Even if they're trying to help sell War Bonds.*

The hospital floor was quiet again. In the stillness, Molly suddenly heard a voice whisper, "Psssst! Girl!"

4

THE CLUE AT THE HOSPITAL

Startled, Molly scanned the hall. No one else was in sight. The door to Room 201 was open, and the voice seemed to come from in there. Molly stepped across the hall and peeked into the room.

The only occupant was a plump woman with fluffy white hair and alert blue eyes. She sat in bed, propped up by pillows. On the table next to her were several pictures in silver frames, and a china teacup in a saucer. The elderly woman smiled at Molly. "You must be one of the new volunteers, aren't you, dear?"

"Yes, ma'am," Molly answered automatically. Then she remembered that she was just a magazine girl. "Well, sort of," she added.

She held out the *Ladies' Home Journal.* "Would you like a magazine to read?"

"No, thank you," said the woman, and then she nodded at the empty cup on her bedside table. "But I wonder if you would be so kind as to get me a cup of tea? I'm rather thirsty."

Molly thought for a moment. Mr. Pritchard had warned her against bothering patients, but surely he wouldn't mind if she *helped* a patient. "I'll go ask the nurse," said Molly, picking up the teacup.

"A spoonful of sugar, please, and just a touch of milk," the elderly woman called after her as Molly left the room.

The second-floor hall was still empty, but Molly heard the jangling bottles of the medicine cart on the first floor. She went downstairs and explained to Nurse Schroeder that the lady in 201 had asked for a cup of tea.

"Mrs. Currier *always* wants her cup of tea," said the nurse with a sigh. "She doesn't seem to realize that we have other patients to care for, too." She glanced at the teacup in Molly's hand.

"If you want to get it for her, you'll have to go yourself. Take the service stairs down to the kitchen," she added, pointing toward the end of the hall, "and ask Marta to help you."

Following the nurse's directions, Molly went to the end of the hall, opened a door marked "To Kitchen," and took a flight of stairs to the basement. Sniffing the warm smell of bread baking, she walked down a short hall and through a pair of swinging doors into the hospital's kitchen.

Inside the well-scrubbed kitchen, a woman was kneading dough on a large wooden table. Molly recognized her as the aide who had been mopping the lobby earlier. A little girl about six years old sat on a tall stool by the table. She was looking at a book, but she glanced up when Molly came in. She had pale skin, dark brown hair braided in pigtails, and wide brown eyes. She looked so much like the aide that Molly was sure she must be the woman's daughter.

"Can I help you?" the aide asked. Molly

explained Mrs. Currier's request, remembering to mention the spoonful of sugar and the splash of milk.

The aide nodded and then disappeared into what looked like a storage pantry at the back of the kitchen. While Molly waited, she noticed that the little girl was watching her. Molly smiled at her. The girl shyly smiled back, then quickly bent her head over her book again.

The aide came back carrying a small teapot. She set it on a tray with the cup and saucer. She was reaching into a canister labeled "Sugar" when a man wearing a chef's hat came through the swinging doors. "Marta!" he shouted. "What are you doing?"

In her thick accent, Marta told him that she was preparing a cup of tea for Mrs. Currier.

"No!" the chef exploded, his face red with anger. "Too much sugar is disappearing from my kitchen."

Molly tensed. Was sugar missing here, too?

She watched the chef grab the canister and carry it into the pantry. "From now on, no one will get extra helpings unless I say so," he declared. Pulling a ring of keys from his pocket, he locked the pantry. Then he stormed out a door at the back of the room.

As the sound of the banging door echoed through the kitchen, Marta took a deep breath. Her dark eyes looked troubled. She poured a splash of milk into Mrs. Currier's cup and then, without a word, handed the tray to Molly.

Molly carefully carried the tea tray up the two flights of stairs to Room 201. As she set the tray down on Mrs. Currier's bedside table, one of the silver-framed pictures caught her eye. It was a photo of a well-dressed couple standing in front of an elegant stone house. "Greystone Manor!" Molly exclaimed, peering closely at the picture.

"Yes, indeed," said Mrs. Currier. She picked up the photo and smiled proudly at it. "That's a picture of my late husband, Trevor, and myself. It was taken almost thirty years ago. And that's my home, Greystone Manor. Do you live nearby?"

"Not exactly," said Molly. "I live on Oak Street."

"Oak Street?" Mrs. Currier repeated thoughtfully. "Perhaps you know Dr. and Mrs. McIntire?"

Molly grinned. "They're my parents."

"What a small world!" exclaimed Mrs. Currier. "Your mother and I served on a library committee together. I remember having a meeting at your house. And your father is one of the finest physicians in Jefferson. You must be very proud of him!"

"Yes, ma'am, I am," Molly agreed. "He's in the Army now, taking care of wounded soldiers in England."

"Ah, so many things have changed," said Mrs. Currier sadly. "My dear nephew is in the Army, too. He's stationed somewhere in Europe. All my other relatives are now far away, too."

Mrs. Currier was silent for a moment, and Molly didn't quite know what to say next. *What would it be like,* she wondered, *to be old and sick and all alone?*

Then Mrs. Currier sighed and put back the photo. "It's been a long time since I've been able to go home. I do miss my house so, and all the things in it." Then she looked up at Molly. "You know, there's one thing I especially miss. Perhaps you could help me with it."

"I'll try," offered Molly, smiling.

Mrs. Currier explained that she had broken her reading glasses. "I have another pair at home but no way to get them. Would you go get them for me?"

Molly's smile vanished. "You mean, go inside Greystone Manor?"

"It would take you just a few minutes," said Mrs. Currier, caught up in her plan. "And I'll tell you exactly where the glasses are." There was a gleam of excitement in her blue eyes. "Oh, it would be so wonderful to be able to read again. And I could enjoy the magazine you were so kind to offer."

With a sinking heart, Molly found herself agreeing to Mrs. Currier's request. "But I'll have to ask my mother for permission," she cautioned.

"I'm sure your mother won't mind you doing this little errand for me," Mrs. Currier said confidently. She told Molly how to find the house key and the spare glasses, and then she asked when Molly would be back.

"Um, we'll be here again on Thursday," said Molly, backing out of the hospital room.

"I'll look forward to seeing you then!" Mrs. Currier exclaimed.

Outside the room, Molly found Emily waiting in the sitting area. "What's wrong?" Emily whispered. "You look ill."

"I'll tell you outside," Molly whispered back.

As they crossed the lawn to their bicycles, Molly told Emily about her promise to Mrs. Currier. She hoped that Emily would offer to go with her, but Emily looked worried.

"It *is* rather lonely up there," Emily said as they wheeled their bicycles to the road. "You wouldn't go at night, would you?"

Molly shuddered. "Not a chance!"

5

A Disappearing Act

Molly had been hungry all afternoon, but at dinner that night she found that she could barely swallow a bite. *Why did I ever tell Mrs. Currier that I'd go into that spooky old house?* she worried as she picked at the cheese on top of her soybean casserole. *I must have been crazy!*

She hoped that her mother wouldn't allow her to go to Greystone Manor—or, at the very least, would insist on going with her. But Molly hadn't yet had a chance to talk with her mother. Mrs. McIntire was working late at the Red Cross, so Mrs. Gilford, the McIntires' housekeeper, had served dinner and then gone home, leaving Jill in charge.

Usually, Jill enjoyed being the boss of the

house, but tonight she just sat in her chair, toying with her salad and saying nothing. She didn't even complain about the soybean casserole, which she'd often before described as "unfit for human consumption." And when the radio started broadcasting news about the latest battle in Europe, Jill got up and turned it off.

"Aw!" protested Ricky. "I wanted to hear that! Maybe they would've mentioned the planes they're using. I could've told you all about 'em."

Ricky was training to become a volunteer plane spotter, and he loved showing off his new knowledge at the dinner table. "Today I got this book on the different types of planes," he said excitedly. "And once I pass the plane spotter test, I'm gonna get assigned two-hour shifts when I'll watch all the planes that fly over us. I'll look at each one and say whether it has one or two engines, how high it's flying, and where it's heading."

Six-year-old Brad was playing with his

favorite toy, a tiny model airplane. "Zoom, zoom!" Brad shouted as he flew his plane toward Ricky's dinner plate.

Ricky looked at Brad's plane. "That one right there is a B-17 bomber. That's an American plane, so that would be okay. But if it was an enemy plane, I'd call in an alert, so we could shoot it down before it dropped any bombs on us."

"Boom!" yelled Brad, pretending to drop a bomb on his cheese-covered soybeans. "Ka-bang!!"

Emily hunched over her plate, and Molly remembered how her friend had lived through real bombings. "Stop it, Brad," Molly told her brother.

Ricky was describing different enemy planes in detail when Mrs. McIntire came home. She looked tired, but she listened carefully as Ricky told her all about the differences between the American and German bombers. "I'm proud of you," she told him. "You're obviously taking your new responsibility very seriously."

"Yeah!" Ricky agreed. "Wouldn't it be great if I spotted a German plane flying right over Jefferson!" Ricky pretended he had a machine gun in his hands and was firing at an enemy plane in the sky. "Rat-a-tat-tat!"

"Rat-a-tat-tat!" Brad imitated him delightedly.

"No, it wouldn't be great," said Jill suddenly. She threw down her napkin in disgust. "Don't you know that war is real? And people are getting wounded and killed every day!"

"Gee," said Ricky. "I was only kidding."

But Jill continued as if she hadn't even heard him. "I was at the hospital today, and they assigned us to serve coffee to some of the wounded soldiers. One boy was only eighteen, and he'd lost his right arm. And there was another whose eyes were so badly burned that he may never see again." Jill shook her head as if she were trying to shake away the memory. "I—I felt so sorry for them, and all I could do was offer a cup of coffee and..."

Tears started rolling down Jill's cheeks. She

jumped up from the table and ran out of the room. Mrs. McIntire followed her.

The rest of the meal was eaten in silence. After dinner, it was Molly's turn to help with the dishes. She was in the kitchen, scraping soybean casserole from the plates, when her mother came back in. "Jill will be all right," her mother assured her.

Mrs. McIntire put on her apron and said she was sorry she'd had to work so late. "We're all working extra hours to get everything ready for the canteen," she said as she began to wash the dishes. "We have so much to do before Saturday."

"Did you find out where the sugar is?"

"Not all of it," Mrs. McIntire said. "So far, I've learned that two of the bags were given to another Red Cross chapter. And one bag was used to make refreshments for a blood donor drive. I still don't know what's happened to the other four bags, though. And as we checked all the supplies, we discovered we're also missing quite a bit of coffee, some of the cooking oil we use for frying doughnuts, and a few other things, too."

Molly frowned. She remembered what the chef at Oak Knoll Hospital had said about sugar disappearing from his kitchen. She told her mother about it. "Don't you think it's strange that sugar is missing from both places?"

"Well, even with the best of intentions, people can become careless," Mrs. McIntire said as she scrubbed. "At the Red Cross, a volunteer may have taken out the sugar for a good reason, but forgot to record it."

Molly did some quick arithmetic. If there were four sacks of sugar missing, and each sack weighed ten pounds, that meant forty pounds of sugar was gone. *That's an awful lot of sugar to forget about,* she thought.

"Could thieves be stealing the sugar— maybe so they could sell it on the black market?" asked Molly, remembering her conversation with Emily.

"Don't let your imagination run away with you, olly Molly," her mother said with a smile. "Sugar *is* valuable right now, but why would a thief steal only four sacks—and leave one on the shelf? Besides, the volunteers are all trustworthy people. I would hate to suspect any of them.

"I'm still hopeful that we'll find the missing supplies somewhere," Mrs. McIntire continued. "But in the meantime, I have to figure out how we're going to get all the cookies we need for the canteen on Saturday."

Molly wiped the dishes in silence, but she kept thinking about the missing sugar. She knew that the halls of the Red Cross were usually busy with visitors as well as volunteers, and the storeroom wasn't always locked. *Just about anyone could've taken the sugar,* she thought. *And maybe they didn't have time to steal it all, so they only took some of the sacks.*

Her mother handed her the silverware and asked, "How was your first day as a magazine delivery girl?"

"All right, I suppose," said Molly, drying the knives, forks, and spoons and putting them in the drawer. "But I wish I got to do something important instead. Jill is a real hospital volunteer, and Ricky is going to be a plane spotter. All I get to do is hand out dumb old magazines."

"I understand how you feel," Mrs. McIntire said as she rinsed the last dishes. "But everything we do to help other people is important. I'd bet some of the patients you visited today have family members in the military, don't they?"

Molly nodded.

"Well," continued her mother, "by helping those patients, you're also helping everyone in their families, including the men fighting overseas."

"I guess so," Molly said reluctantly. She closed the silverware drawer with unnecessary force. "But if only Emily didn't want to go visit her aunt all the time, we could've both joined the JFA instead."

"Imagine if you were in a strange country, staying with a strange family, and your

Aunt Eleanor were somewhere nearby," Mrs. McIntire suggested. "Don't you think you'd want to visit your aunt, too?"

"That would be different," said Molly, adding to herself, *Aunt Eleanor is nice, not at all like an 'Auntie Prim'!* Then Molly thought about her mother's words again. "Do you think Emily wishes she weren't living with us?" she asked. "Do we seem strange to her?"

"I meant 'strange' in the sense that we're different, not bad," her mother explained. "And I don't think Emily is unhappy here. But it's only natural that she should miss her home and family."

"Oh," said Molly, feeling disappointment like a lump in her stomach. *I thought Emily and I were really friends. But maybe she's only being nice because she has to live here with us.*

Mrs. McIntire finished wiping out the sink. "Thanks for helping me in the kitchen," she told Molly. "Now I'd better go tuck Brad into bed."

"Wait," said Molly as her mother turned to leave. "There's something I wanted to ask you about." She told her mother about Mrs. Currier's request that she go to Greystone Manor and get the glasses. "She said that she knows you," Molly added.

"We were on a committee together," said Mrs. McIntire. "Mrs. Currier used to be one of Jefferson's leading citizens. She was always busy helping people and running things. I didn't know she was in the hospital. I really should go visit her."

"Is it all right with you if I go to her house tomorrow?" Molly asked doubtfully. "I mean, it'll be empty and everything."

"Hmm," said Mrs. McIntire as she untied her apron. She paused for a moment, as if she was thinking.

Molly could hear the kitchen clock ticking.

Finally, her mother said, "I think you're grown-up enough to do this kind of errand now. Unless, of course, you don't want to."

"I guess I don't mind," Molly said, trying to sound casual.

"All right then," said Mrs. McIntire. "You

can go after school tomorrow. Just be sure you're home in time for dinner."

Molly was left standing in the kitchen with a damp dishtowel hanging from her hand. As she thought about going into Greystone Manor all by herself, she remembered everything she'd ever heard about spooky old houses. With a shudder, she imagined spiders dangling from the ceilings, and mice scurrying everywhere. And there might be ghosts who walked on creaking floorboards in the night, moaning softly...

No! Molly told herself firmly. *I'm not even going to think about ghosts.*

But as she hung up the dishtowel and turned off the kitchen lights, Molly remembered the eerie light she'd seen in the cellar of Greystone Manor. Someone—or something—had turned off that light. And if it wasn't a ghost, what was it?

6

UNEXPECTED VISITORS

The next day, Molly was prepared to beg
Emily to go to Greystone Manor with her. She
was relieved to discover that Emily had been
planning to go all the time.

"Of course," said Emily in her quiet way.
"You signed up to be a magazine girl with me."

After school, the girls went home and
quickly walked Bennett and Yank. It was a cool,
cloudy afternoon, and Molly kept hoping for
a storm so ferocious that she couldn't possibly
be expected to go to Greystone Manor. The sky,
however, refused to spill even a drop of rain.
"I guess we'd better go," she said finally.

They pulled their bikes out of the garage
and started off for Overlook Hill. Molly had to
slow down occasionally so that she didn't leave

Emily too far behind, but Emily was beginning
to be more comfortable on a bike. The girls were
able to ride most of the way up Overlook Hill.
Near the top of the hill, they parked their bikes
under pine trees by the side of the road. Then
they walked up the last section.

Maybe this won't be so bad, Molly told herself
when they reached the driveway that led to
Greystone Manor. *I'll pretend it's like when I go to
the Pedersons' to feed their cats.* But the Pedersons
lived just a few houses away from the McIntires.
Molly could even see her house from the Pedersons' kitchen window. All she could see around
Greystone Manor were trees.

The manor house itself looked even bigger
than Molly had remembered. Four huge chim-
neys sat on the ridge of the sharply slanted
roof. Beneath the roof, about a dozen darkened
windows faced an empty lawn. There were
flower boxes at the windows, but all the flowers
had died long ago. Now just a few withered
vines straggled down the front of the house.

Molly surveyed the house carefully, checking

to see whether there were any more mysterious lights glowing in the cellar. Everything looked dark. As she wondered again where the strange light had come from, she felt a shiver run up her spine.

"Are you all right?" asked Emily.

Molly forced herself to smile. "Sure. Why?"

"Well, you just shook yourself like this," said Emily, giving an imitation that looked like the puppies shaking off their baths.

"I'm just cold," said Molly. She glanced up at the gray sky. It was still stubbornly refusing to rain. *I've got to be tough,* she told herself.

Out loud Molly said, "We have to go over there first." She pointed to a small, two-story building next to the house. "Mrs. Currier said it used to be a stable, but now it's a garage, and that's where she keeps her spare key."

Emily nodded. "All right, let's go."

The two girls half-walked, half-ran down the driveway. They were out of breath when they reached the garage's wide wooden doors, which swung out like stable doors. Molly put her hand on one door, and then paused. "This place has been empty a long time. There could be spiders everywhere. Or mice."

Emily took a step back. "Mice don't really bother me," she said, frowning. "But I'm not at all fond of spiders. Why don't we open the door with a stick and see what's inside?"

"All right," said Molly. "And I don't mind spiders that much. So if it's spiders, I'll go in first, and if it's mice, you can go in first."

Together, the girls found a long stick and pried the door open. Then they stood back at a safe distance and peered in.

"Doesn't look too bad," said Molly hopefully. "Just a few cobwebs." She ventured inside, with Emily just behind her. "It smells like gasoline, though!"

The old stable was big enough to hold two cars, but there was only one parked inside—a big old black Packard that looked as if it hadn't been driven in years. Several shovels and rakes hung on hooks near the door. Molly searched behind the shovels on the last hook and found, as Mrs. Currier had promised, an old-fashioned iron key hanging on a length of twine.

"Got it!" she told Emily. They hurried out of the garage and over to the tall front door of the house. Molly had to try the key several times before the door's rusty lock gave way. Emily twisted the brass doorknob, and suddenly they were inside the house.

"It's dark in here, isn't it?" said Molly as she shut the door behind them and thrust the key into her jacket pocket. Her voice was just above a whisper. Somehow it didn't seem right to talk loudly inside this silent house.

"I guess it's because all the curtains are closed," Emily agreed as they walked down the hall. A little light filtered through the silky curtains, and the girls could see a book-lined study on their left, followed by a music room with a grand piano. On their right was a wide living room with a long couch and several armchairs. Beyond the living room was a dining room with a table that looked big enough for twenty people.

"I don't think anyone's been here for quite a long time," added Emily as they passed the musty-smelling rooms.

They reached the staircase at the end of the shadowy hall. "We go up here," Molly whispered. "Mrs. Currier said her glasses are in her bedroom, in the top drawer of her writing desk."

The girls climbed the stairs to the second floor and found themselves in a hall even darker than the main floor. The only light came through an octagonal stained-glass window at the end of the hall. Closed doors lined the hallway.

"Which door?" asked Emily.

Molly shrugged. "She just said her bedroom. I didn't think to ask which room that was."

Staying very close together, the girls opened the doors one by one. They found a sewing room, a bathroom, a linen closet that smelled of mothballs, and a room with two twin beds but no writing desk.

Finally, the girls opened the door to a

spacious room with a canopy bed. Blue silk brocade covered the bed, and matching blue silk curtains draped the tall windows. In the far corner of the room, near the windows, stood an elegant writing desk with several silver-framed pictures on it.

"This must be it," said Molly.

She went over to the desk and opened the top drawer. There, just as Mrs. Currier had said, was a brown leather case with a pair of wire-rimmed glasses inside. Molly stuck the case into her jacket pocket. "We can go!"

They were halfway across the room when Molly heard the crackling of gravel outside. Emily sucked in her breath. "What's that?"

Molly listened hard. The sound was getting louder. "I don't know," she whispered. She crossed back to the windows, lifted a corner of the silk curtain, and peeked outside. She saw a black truck driving toward the house.

Molly dropped the curtain as if it were on fire. "Someone's coming!"

7

THE KEY

Outside, a truck door slammed.

"We have to hide!" Emily whispered, her eyes wide with fear.

There was a narrow space between the canopy bed and the windows. Emily slipped into it, crouching on the floor. Molly squeezed in beside her and tucked herself into a tight ball. She felt cold all over, but her hands were damp with sweat.

I've always wondered what people meant by "cold sweat," Molly thought. *Now I know.*

Together, the girls waited and waited, listening hard. All they could hear was their own breathing. "Do you think they left?" Emily whispered finally.

Molly crawled to the window. Peeking

under the curtain again, she had a clear view of the driveway. "I don't see the truck."

Emily looked, too. "I don't see it either. Let's go."

Cautiously, the two girls began to inch their way out of the room. When they reached the doorway, Molly looked up and down the hall. The dim shadows seemed more threatening than ever.

"Do you see anything?" asked Emily.

Molly shook her head. Then she took a deep breath and launched herself out of the doorway. Emily followed her. They tiptoed toward the staircase at the end of the hall, going as fast as they could without making too much noise.

At the top of the stairs, Molly stopped. She remembered someone telling her that the center of a step usually creaked the most. She stayed close to the wall as she started down the steps, motioning to Emily to do the same.

When the girls reached the first floor,

they started down the long hallway toward the front door. As they were tiptoeing past the living room, a loud crash sounded.

Both girls froze. They could hear the sound of footsteps below them in the cellar. "Last ones coming in," a man's voice said. Then there was the heavy tread of someone climbing stairs.

They're coming up here! thought Molly, her heart pounding.

Emily grabbed Molly's arm, and together they ran into the living room and dove behind the long couch. Waiting in the dim room, Molly heard a man's muffled voice say, "Well, we'll be done by Saturday."

A door banged somewhere in the cellar. Then, a few minutes later, Molly heard an engine start up outside. Molly crept over to the window behind the couch. Peering out, she caught a glimpse of the black truck speeding up the driveway.

"They're driving away!" she told Emily. As soon as the sound of crackling gravel faded, both girls jumped to their feet. They flew out the front door and slammed it behind them.

Without a word, they raced up the steep driveway, and then down the hill to the tree-shaded spot where they had parked their bicycles. The wind blew hard in Molly's face as she sped down the hill on her bike, with Emily close behind.

The girls didn't stop until they reached Lincoln Park. Then they dropped their bikes on the ground and collapsed on the grass. "I've never been so scared in my entire life," Molly said when she could finally talk.

Emily nodded. "When we heard that truck, all I could think of was to hide. Just as we do at home in the bombings."

"I'm glad we did hide!" exclaimed Molly. "There's something creepy about that house! First we see the light there, and then we hear those men. What if—"

But before she could finish her sentence, Ricky strolled over with his friend David. "What's the matter with you two?" Ricky asked, casually tossing a ball into the air and catching it with his baseball mitt. "You look like you've seen a ghost or something."

Molly sat up. "It was worse than a ghost!" she blurted out. "I told Mrs. Currier I'd go get her glasses for her, so we had to go into Greystone Manor."

With help from Emily, Molly told her brother what had happened inside the house. She expected Ricky to be amazed. But when she finished her story, he was still tossing and catching his baseball.

"Well," said Molly, irritated. "Don't you think that's scary?"

"No!" said Ricky. "I think you girls are dumb to get so excited. What'd the truck look like?"

Feeling like a real detective, Molly tried to remember it exactly. "It was about the size of the milkman's truck," she said slowly. "And it was closed in back like the milkman's truck, but it was black and you couldn't see inside it at all."

David spoke up. "Sounds like a repair-man's truck."

"They could've been working on the fur-nace or something," suggested Ricky, calmly catching his baseball again.

"Yeah," David agreed. "Some guys just came and worked in the cellar, and then left." He shrugged. "Big deal."

The two boys turned away and walked back to the baseball diamond together. Molly and Emily looked at each other. "Do you think it was just repairmen?" Molly asked her friend.

"No," said Emily, frowning. "But I can't really say why."

For several long minutes, Molly sat hunched over on the ground, plucking blades of grass as she thought about the mysterious truck. Suddenly she sat up straight, her eyes bright. "When we looked out the window, we didn't see the truck in the driveway and we thought it was gone, right?" she asked Emily.

"Yes," said Emily. "It must have still been there, though, because later we heard the men downstairs. And then we saw the truck drive away."

"Right!" Molly exclaimed. "So if the truck was still at the house, but it wasn't anywhere in the driveway, it must have been in the garage."

"So?"

"Usually, only the people who live in the house will park in the garage," said Molly excitedly. "Repairmen always park in the drive-way or on the street. Isn't it the same way in London?"

"I suppose," Emily said hesitantly.

"So I don't think it was repairmen at all," Molly concluded. "And whoever it was, I don't know why they parked in the garage. It was like they were trying to hide their truck."

"Perhaps it was a cleaner," Emily suggested sensibly. "Someone who comes to the house every week, and always parks in the same place. The garage did smell of petrol, and it looked as if someone had been using it."

"Petrol? Oh, that's what you call gas, isn't it? Yes, it did." Molly picked a few more blades of grass. "But I don't think cleaners have been in that house for a long time. Mrs. Gilford would've had a fit if she'd seen all the dust in there."

"It *was* dusty," Emily agreed. "When we were hiding behind the sofa, I was terribly afraid I was going to sneeze."

For a few minutes, the girls considered other possibilities. Emily suggested that perhaps the truck belonged to friends of Mrs. Currier who came by to check on the house.

"If she has friends who visit the house, then why did she ask me to get her glasses for her?" Molly objected. Thinking of the glasses, she reached into her pocket to reassure herself that they were still there. She felt the leather eyeglass case, but there was something else there, too.

"Oh no!"

"What?" demanded Emily.

Molly pulled out an old-fashioned key hanging from a piece of twine. "I forgot to leave the key!"

Emily stared at the iron key as if it were a snake poised to bite. "I suppose we have to take it back, don't we?"

A few fat raindrops started to fall. Molly stood up and glanced at the darkening sky. "Not now. It's too late. I promised my mom we'd be home for dinner. We could take it back tomorrow, though, as soon as school is out."

Emily got to her feet, too. "Tomorrow we're going to Oak Knoll again."

A raindrop landed on Molly's glasses. "Then we can take it on Friday," Molly said.

"At least we won't have to go inside the house again," said Emily, looking nervous.

"We *could* just leave the key, but maybe we should look around a little bit," Molly said slowly. "I think something strange is going on at that house—and I want to show Ricky he's not nearly as smart as he thinks he is."

8
A THREAT

After school on Thursday, Molly and Emily picked up their magazines at the Red Cross and rode over to Oak Knoll. Remembering Mr. Pritchard's instructions, they parked their bikes behind the hospital, near the delivery entrance.

The girls were hurrying through the hospital with their magazines when Molly ran straight into Mr. Pritchard. Her magazines fell to the floor and scattered across the hallway.

"Watch where you're going, young lady!" Mr. Pritchard reprimanded her.

"I *was* watching, sir," Molly tried to explain as she pushed her glasses back into place. Her face felt hot with embarrassment. "I just wasn't watching where *you* were going."

A Threat

"Don't be impertinent," Mr. Pritchard
snapped. "Remember, this is a new program.
If you girls cause problems, the magazine
deliveries will be discontinued."

Emily had bent down to gather the fallen
magazines. Now she looked up. "The patients
seem to like the magazines," she said shyly.

"We're a convalescent hospital, not a recre-
ation hall," Mr. Pritchard told her. "Keep in
mind that our patients need rest and quiet."
He stared down at the girls' shoes. "And wipe
your feet!"

As Mr. Pritchard strode off down the hall,
Molly and Emily went back to the entrance
and wiped their shoes on the doormat. "Why
does he always yell at us?" Molly muttered
as they made their way back down the hall.
"We're just trying to help."

"Auntie Prim says he acts like an army
officer, the way he orders his staff about.
And he looks as if he always has a headache."
Emily imitated Mr. Pritchard's scowl, and
Molly giggled.

"But," Emily added, "Auntie Prim also says that he keeps everything very clean, and she likes that."

Molly looked around the gleaming hospital. The floors were shiny and there wasn't a speck of dust on the woodwork. A nurse in a starched white uniform was striding quickly down the hall, and the man from Laurence Laundry was delivering stacks of crisply ironed sheets.

"It *is* clean," she admitted. "Why does Mr. Pritchard have to be so mean, though?"

The nurse eyed Molly and Emily, as if to ask why they were standing around talking. The girls quickly went up the stairs to begin their deliveries.

As she visited the second-floor rooms, Molly discovered that many of the patients remembered her. "Oh, good!" said Mr. Emory in Room 203. "I was hoping you'd come back. I just got a letter from my oldest son—would you like to hear it?"

Molly saved a copy of *National Geographic*

for the boy in Room 214, but he snorted with disgust when he saw it. "I've already read that one!" he complained. "Don't you have any others?"

I don't care if he is sick, he's awfully grouchy, thought Molly. "No," she told him shortly. "That's the only one I have left. Do you want a *Time* or a *Ladies' Home Journal* instead?"

"I suppose I'll take the *Time*," he said, but he sounded disappointed. He turned his face as far as he could toward Molly, and she noticed how thin he was. "Will you read me something about the Army? My dad's in the Army somewhere in England right now."

"So's my dad," Molly told him. She glanced at the *Time.* "I guess I could read one article."

As Molly searched the magazine for a story about the Army, the boy began talking. He said his name was Phillip, he was eight years old, and when he grew up he was going to be an Army spy. "My back might not ever be strong enough for me to be a regular soldier," he explained. "But I'm going to sneak behind enemy lines and find out everything they're doing."

He lowered his voice to a whisper. "I know everything that goes on at this hospital right now—I even know someone who's breaking the rules and could get into a lot of trouble!"

It's not hard to break the rules around here, Molly thought. *Every time I come here, I get into trouble.* But she decided to humor the boy. "I bet you'll make a great spy someday," she told him. She showed him a one-page article on the Army's fighting in Italy. "Want to hear this?"

Phillip nodded. As Molly read the news story aloud, he listened with intense concentration. When she'd finished, he asked her to read another article, but Molly explained that she had more patients to visit.

"Come back next time," Phillip ordered as she was leaving. "And bring a new *National Geographic.*"

Molly saved Mrs. Currier's room for last. When she showed Mrs. Currier the eyeglass case, the old lady beamed. "Bless you, my dear!" she exclaimed.

Mrs. Currier put the glasses on and looked at one of Molly's magazines. "Before, it was all just a blur, but now I can see every word. I can't thank you enough!"

"Oh," Molly said modestly. "It was nothing. My friend Emily helped me, too."

"You didn't have any trouble finding them, did you?" asked Mrs. Currier.

Molly remembered the frightening events of the previous afternoon. "Not really," she fibbed. Then her conscience made her confess, "But I'm sorry, I forgot to lock the door and leave the key when we left. We were sort of, um, in a hurry."

Mrs. Currier looked quite concerned. "Oh, dear!" she said. "Can you go back and lock it this afternoon?"

Molly hesitated. It was getting late, and she did *not* want to go back to Greystone Manor in the dark. "I can't go back today, but I could go tomorrow," she offered.

"I suppose it would be all right to leave it unlocked for just one more day," said Mrs. Currier reluctantly. "Are you sure you'll go tomorrow?"

"Yes, ma'am."

Mrs. Currier began to pepper her with questions about the house. "How does it look?"

"Um, fine," said Molly, and then she searched for something else to say. "It's very big, isn't it?"

"Ah, yes! Trevor and I used to love to entertain. Such fun we had! And are the trees as beautiful as ever?"

"There are a lot of trees, and they are very tall," Molly said truthfully. Then she decided to ask something she'd been wondering about. "Does anyone else live at the house?"

"No," said Mrs. Currier with a sigh. "We used to have a very nice couple, the Swensons, who were our chauffeur and our housekeeper. They lived in the apartment over the garage. But when I became ill, the house had to be shut up, and the Swensons took a job in California."

She sighed again. "I wish I did have someone keeping an eye on the property."

If no one is living at the house, who was there yesterday? Molly wondered. She didn't want to worry Mrs. Currier, but she decided to risk another question. "Is it hard to get repairs done on the house—I mean, if no one is living there now?"

Mrs. Currier shook her head. "I've given up worrying about repairs, dear. That will all have to wait until I'm well enough to go home."

Ricky was wrong! Molly thought with a flash of triumph. *It wasn't repairmen!* Then she felt a chill of fear. *But who was it?*

Before Molly could ask any more questions, Nurse Schroeder came in with Mrs. Currier's medicine. "Ah," said Mrs. Currier, smiling hopefully at Molly, "a nice cup of tea would certainly make this medicine go down better."

Molly glanced at the nurse. "You can ask for it down in the kitchen," Nurse Schroeder said. Molly started for the door.

"And just a sliver of cake to go with the tea, please," Mrs. Currier called after her.

Molly went down the two flights of stairs to the hospital kitchen. The hall outside the kitchen smelled like fresh-baked cornbread today. Inside the swinging doors, Molly saw the aide, Marta, cutting squares of the yellow bread and putting each square on a bread plate. Marta's daughter was sitting on a stool at the table. She was helping her mother by placing a spoonful of red jam next to each piece of cornbread.

The little girl looked up at Molly and smiled shyly before returning to her work. Molly smiled back, and then she explained to the aide that Mrs. Currier had asked for a cup of tea. Without a word, Marta made up a tea tray, remembering to add a dash of milk to the cup.

"Thank you," Molly said.

The aide nodded formally. "You are welcome," she said in her thick accent, and then she returned to the cornbread.

A THREAT

Molly had climbed the first flight of stairs before she remembered that Mrs. Currier had asked for cake, too. *If they don't have cake, maybe she'd like a piece of cornbread with jam,* Molly thought.

She turned around and headed back downstairs. Just before she reached the swinging doors, she heard a loud, angry voice inside the kitchen.

"You and your kid shouldn't even be here," a man was saying. "And if you cause any trouble, I'll tell the cops about you!"

9

A DISTURBING DISCOVERY

Shocked, Molly stopped just outside the kitchen door. She heard a woman talking in a low tone and, although she couldn't make out the words, she was sure it was Marta's voice.

What's Marta done? Molly wondered. *Why is someone threatening to tell the police about her?*

Molly decided this was not the time to ask for a piece of cake. She hurried back down the hall. She was halfway up the stairs when the man from Laurence Laundry flung open the kitchen doors. In a few long strides, he climbed past her on the stairs. Then he stopped and turned around. Molly could see the name "Mr. Laurence" embroidered in red thread on the pocket of his blue uniform. He looked at Molly questioningly. "Did you hear what happened in there, young lady?"

Molly nodded.

"Well, I'm sorry I got angry," Mr. Laurence said. He took a deep breath and seemed to steady himself. "But we're in the middle of a war now, and we've got to be careful."

Mr. Laurence looked around the empty stairwell and then lowered his voice. "Some people, especially foreigners, can't always be trusted. That's all I'll say for now. But," he added with a glance back at the kitchen, "be on the lookout for anything suspicious, you understand?"

Before Molly could think of an answer, Mr. Laurence hurried on. As she carried the tea tray up to the second floor, Molly felt her stomach knot. *Could Marta really be a criminal?* she wondered.

Molly's hands were trembling as she poured the tea for Mrs. Currier. "I'm sorry, but I couldn't get cake," she apologized.

"That's all right, dear," said Mrs. Currier. She patted Molly's arm gently. "I didn't really expect it. We never seem to get nice cakes any-more. One of the nurses said something about the kitchen running short of sugar. I suppose it's this awful war."

Or, Molly wondered, *is there a thief at Oak Knoll?*

★

That night at dinner, Mrs. McIntire reported that the sugar missing from the Red Cross still had not been found. "There's enough sugar for coffee and cocoa for Saturday's canteen, but not nearly enough to make all the cookies."

"Can't you skip the cookies?" suggested Ricky. "Just this once?"

"Well," said Mrs. McIntire slowly, "we had a meeting, and we considered that possibility—"

"No! You can't do that!" Jill broke in. Surprised by her outburst, everyone turned to her.

"I've heard patients talk about the cookies," continued Jill, her face flushed with emotion.

"One soldier said his train stopped at Glennings a year ago, just as he was about to go overseas. He still remembers how nice the volunteers were and how they welcomed him and his buddies with coffee and fresh-baked cookies. He said it was like a taste of home."

Jill looked around the table. "Don't you see?" she asked. "The cookies make a difference."

"Yes," said Mrs. McIntire quietly. "That's what we decided, too. The cookies are an important Jefferson tradition, and we're going to go ahead with it, no matter what. I've been put in charge of getting as many cookies as possible for Saturday, and I'm going to need your help."

Brad spoke up. "The soldiers can have my dinner," he offered. "And my breakfast, too!"

"That's very generous, Brad," Mrs. McIntire said, patting his head. "But what we really need now is sugar. I'm asking all the ladies I know if they can bake a few dozen cookies. Mrs. Gilford and I are going to bake, too." Mrs. McIntire paused, and then added, "We plan to use up all the family's sugar for the month. I hope you don't mind."

"The soldiers need it more than we do," Jill said firmly, and Ricky, Emily, and Brad all jumped in with their approval of the plan. Molly glanced at the blue china sugar bowl in the center of the table. She really liked having a bit of sugar on her cereal in the morning. But then she thought about the soldiers going to war—and what their lives would be like on the battlefield—and she added her voice to the chorus of approval.

"Thank you," said Mrs. McIntire, smiling. "Your dad would be proud of you."

If only I could find out who's been taking the sugar, maybe I could get it back, thought Molly. *Then Dad would really be proud of me.*

★

That evening, as Molly and Emily walked their puppies, Molly decided that she had to share her suspicions about Marta. She told

Emily everything that had happened that afternoon. "Marta works in the kitchen," she concluded. "So it would be easy for her to steal sugar from Oak Knoll. And anyone can walk into the Red Cross, so she could be stealing from there, too."

Emily looked doubtful. "Auntie Prim says Marta is nice."

"Does your aunt know her?"

"Auntie Prim likes to chat with everyone," Emily explained. "She's told me about all the people at the hospital. She says that Marta works hard to take care of her daughter, Ruth."

Molly remembered little Ruth smiling up at her from the kitchen table. "I don't want to get Marta into trouble," said Molly. "But Mr. Laurence says we should keep an eye on her. And if she's stealing, we have to think of a way to stop her."

The girls discussed what they should do next. "Could you find out more about Marta from your aunt?" Molly asked.

"I think so," Emily said as Bennett and Yank tumbled and nipped at each other on the grass. "Auntie Prim asked me to read her some of the letters I've gotten from home. She wants to know how things are in London for Mum and Dad. Tomorrow, I could take her the letters and ask about Marta, too."

Molly nodded. "That's a good idea. The sooner we find the thief, the sooner we can return the sugar."

"What about you?" Emily asked. "You have to return the key to Greystone Manor tomorrow. You don't want to go by yourself, do you?"

Molly's insides did a flip-flop. She definitely did not want to go by herself, but then she had a thought. "Linda and Susan don't have JFA on Fridays. I'll ask them to go with me."

★

At recess on Friday, Linda and Susan agreed to keep Molly company as far as the top of the driveway to Greystone Manor—but no farther.

"But I have to go down to the house to lock the door and put back the key," Molly protested.

"We'll wait for you," promised Linda, and Susan nodded.

That afternoon, they all bicycled up Overlook Hill together. It was windy, and the branches overhead bent and creaked loudly as the girls pedaled up the road. When they reached the driveway, Molly looked at her friends hopefully. "Are you sure you won't come down with me?"

"We're sure," said Linda. Then she looked at Molly suspiciously. "You're not planning on going *in* the house again, are you?"

"No, not exactly," admitted Molly, who had already considered that possibility. "Mrs. Currier didn't give me permission to go back inside, so I don't think I should. But we could look into the cellar from the windows. Maybe we could find out where that light that we saw came from."

"What if there's a ghost?" said Susan,

looking horrified. "I don't want to go anywhere near a ghost."

"You can look around if you want to," Linda told Molly firmly. "But we'll stay up here."

"Here's my JFA whistle," added Susan, taking the lanyard from around her neck and handing it to Molly. "If you get into trouble, blow on it. We'll go get help."

Her heart pounding, Molly headed down the driveway alone. First, she locked the front door of the house. As soon as she finished, she looked up the driveway to make sure that Linda and Susan were still there. They waved to her as she headed toward the garage.

She opened the garage door and peered inside cautiously. There was no sign of a black truck or any other vehicle besides the dusty old Packard. The dim garage looked the same, but the odor of gasoline was stronger than she remembered it. *It sure smells like someone is using this garage,* she thought as she hung the key back behind the shovels. *But who— and why?*

A Disturbing Discovery

When Molly returned to the fresh air and
sunlight, she took a deep breath. Then she
looked up to where Linda and Susan had been
waiting at the top of the driveway. No one was
there.

"Linda!" she called. "Susan!"

"We're here," said Susan as she and Linda
walked around the side of the garage.

Relief flooded through Molly. "You changed
your minds?"

"Yeah," said Linda, smiling sheepishly.
"We figured that if there was a ghost, it probably would've gotten you by now. Besides, we
want to see what's in the cellar, too."

Molly grinned. "Let's go."

Together, the girls hurried to the side of
the house and clustered around one of the
cellar's narrow windows. Molly crouched
down on the damp ground and tried to look
through the glass. It was so dirty that she
couldn't see anything. She used her handkerchief to wipe away the grime, and then
she cupped her fingers around her eyes and

peered in again. All she could see were some pipes in a dark room.

Linda and Susan looked in, too. "It's just like the stuff that's in my cellar," said Susan, disappointed.

Linda ventured around to the back of the house. "Here's the door to the cellar," she called to Molly and Susan. They followed her and found an old, heavy bulkhead door, set at an angle into the ground. It was secured by a newer-looking chain and padlock.

"Well, I guess we couldn't go down there even if we wanted to," said Susan.

Suddenly, Molly had an idea. She circled around the house, stopping at a small window. She studied it carefully and then glanced up the driveway. "Isn't this the window where we saw the light?"

"I think so," said Susan. "Me, too," Linda agreed, and both girls took a step back.

Molly stared at the window for a moment. She had a jittery feeling in her stomach that reminded her of how she'd felt at summer camp when she had to jump into the freezing-cold lake.

"Here goes," she said finally. Getting down on her stomach, she wiped the window with her handkerchief. Then she peered in. It was hard to see through the dirt-encrusted glass, but she caught a glimpse of what looked like stacks of boxes and large sacks, piled several feet high. "I wonder what those are?"

"Hey, let us look!" said Linda.

Molly inched over to make room for Susan and Linda. "Those bags look like sacks of flour or sugar," said Susan, peering inside the cellar.

"Who'd have enough ration stamps to buy that much sugar?" Linda asked. "Even if you hoarded it for years, you wouldn't have that much."

Molly stood up and looked around uneasily. "To get that much sugar," she said, "you'd have to steal it."

10
SPY MISSION

Molly bicycled home fast. When she arrived, she found Emily in the backyard with Yank and Bennett. As Molly settled herself on the grass beside them, the puppies tried to climb all over her and lick her face.

"Okay, okay!" Molly said, laughing. "Here, go fetch!" She picked up a stick and threw it across the yard.

As the puppies raced off, Molly told Emily what she had seen at Greystone Manor. "There were bags in the cellar that looked like big sacks of flour or sugar. And they were stacked almost as high as the cellar window. Whoever is stealing the supplies could be hiding them in Mrs. Currier's cellar!"

Molly expected her friend to be impressed

by her detective work. But Emily only shrugged. "Mrs. Currier might be just storing things in her cellar," she said. "My parents put all sorts of things in our cellar. At least they used to, before..."

Emily's voice trailed off, and she shivered slightly. Molly knew that she was remembering the terrible bombings in London. Molly decided to steer the conversation to another topic. "How did your visit to your aunt go?" she asked.

"Not well at all," Emily admitted, her shoulders slumped. "I never got to see her." As she threw another stick for the puppies, she told Molly that she had bicycled to the hospital right after school. But as she was leaving her bike in the back parking lot, she'd met Mr. Pritchard, who was about to drive away in his truck.

"He asked me why I was there, and I told him that I was going to visit my aunt. He said that unless I was working as a volunteer, I could come only during regular visiting hours.

And Friday visiting hours don't begin until seven o'clock tonight."

"He's so mean!" Molly exclaimed.

Just then, the back door opened. Molly's mother stepped out, and a tempting smell of cinnamon and ginger drifted from the kitchen. "Who's mean?" Mrs. McIntire asked, offering the girls a small plate of leftover cookie pieces.

"Mr. Pritchard," said Molly. As she munched on the crisp chunks, she told her mother how the hospital director had not allowed Emily to visit her aunt.

"I know Mr. Pritchard," said Mrs. McIntire. "He's a Red Cross volunteer. He can be grumpy sometimes, but that's because he worries so much and he wants everything to be perfect for his patients. It's really very kind of him to allow children to visit at all. Most hospitals won't."

Molly and Emily looked at each other, unconvinced.

"You know," Mrs. McIntire continued, "a friend across town called to say that she's baked cookies for the canteen. I was going to drive over and pick them up tonight. Would you like me to take you to the hospital, Emily, so you can visit your aunt?"

"Yes, please," said Emily, brightening.

"Can I come, too?" asked Molly. She was curious about Aunt Primrose, and there was also someone else at Oak Knoll she wanted to visit. "And can I take one of our old *National Geographics*?"

After dinner, Molly and Emily climbed into the LaSalle sedan and Mrs. McIntire dropped them off at the hospital's front entrance. "I'll be back in about an hour," she said, and then she drove off.

Oak Knoll looked strange and a bit forbidding in the dark. "I hope Mr. Pritchard is gone," Emily said nervously.

"Me, too," said Molly.

The two girls walked quickly up to the

third floor, keeping an eye out for Mr. Pritchard along the way. Emily stopped at Room 303 and knocked at the door.

"Do come in!" said a cheery voice. A slender middle-aged woman with carrot-colored hair and freckles was the only patient in the room. She was sitting up in bed, and she smiled brightly when the girls entered. "Emily! What a lovely surprise!" she greeted them. "And this must be Molly! I'm so very glad to meet you!"

She's not prim at all, Molly decided after a few moments. *I can see why Emily likes her.* The only signs that Aunt Prim had been sick were that her face was very pale, and sometimes, in the middle of a sentence, she would burst out coughing. But she was brimming with enthusiasm for everything, and she thanked Molly heartily for all her hospitality to Emily.

"Your whole family has been so kind," she told Molly. "Once Emily and Yank come to live with me, you and Bennett must visit us. We'll have great fun. I'll make a proper English tea for you, too."

"I'd like that," said Molly, grinning.

Emily read aloud from letters that her parents had sent. Aunt Prim listened with great interest, asking about various neighbors and friends and what had become of them. Molly was surprised to see that Emily, who was usually so quiet at the McIntires' house, chatted eagerly with her aunt.

When Aunt Prim made a joke, Emily laughed so hard that her face turned bright pink. *She never laughs like that at our house,* thought Molly with a twinge of jealousy.

A dark-haired nurse came into the room and looked at the watch she wore pinned on the front of her uniform. "You mustn't tire out the patient," she warned Emily and Molly.

"I'm not tired at all," Aunt Prim protested. "I love having company. And tell me, Nurse Carter, is your baby feeling better?"

"Yes, thank heavens," said the nurse, smiling now. "It was only a cold after all."

When the nurse had left and closed the door behind her, Aunt Prim told them in a low voice that the nurse's youngest child had been ill for two days. "So worrisome for her! And with her husband in the Marines, too."

Aunt Prim really does know everything about everyone, Molly thought. She cleared her throat and looked significantly at Emily. Emily nodded slightly, and then she asked her aunt about the aide, Marta, who worked in the kitchen.

"Oh yes, I know Marta," Aunt Prim said. "In fact, her little girl, Ruth, attends the school where I teach. I'd often seen Marta walking Ruth to kindergarten. And we've chatted several times while I've been here in hospital." Aunt Prim had a fit of coughing, and then she shook her head. "It's a very sad story."

"What happened?" Molly asked.

"Well, you see," Aunt Prim began, "Marta is a refugee from Poland."

"Oh," Molly and Emily said together. Both girls had heard of the terrible things that were happening in that country. "Was Marta escaping the Nazis?" asked Molly.

Aunt Prim nodded. "Her husband was Jewish. He and Marta had been working against the Nazis, so they were both in terrible danger after the invasion. Marta's husband helped her escape with their baby daughter. He was supposed to follow her, but he was captured..." Aunt Prim hesitated for a moment, staring down at her bedcovers. Then she looked up at the girls. "And he was killed."

For a long time, neither girl said a word. Then Emily took a deep breath and asked her aunt if she thought Marta might be in trouble with the police. Aunt Prim looked surprised. "Why would you"—she paused for another fit of coughing—"think such a thing?"

Reluctantly, Molly explained that she had heard Mr. Laurence talk about reporting Marta to the police.

"Well, he should be ashamed of himself! He's probably afraid of anyone foreign, and he's taking out his fear on poor Marta," Aunt Prim said spiritedly. Then she thought for a moment and added, "There is one thing Marta hasn't been quite open about, though."

"What?" the girls asked together.

Aunt Prim explained that Marta had come to Jefferson because she had a cousin here who had invited her to share an apartment. A few months ago, however, Marta's cousin had married a man in the Army and had moved away. Marta couldn't afford the apartment on her own, so she and Ruth were now renting a small room in a nearby town.

"Marta wants to keep Ruth in the Jefferson public school, so she hasn't yet told the school that she's moved to another town," said Aunt Prim. "She keeps hoping that she'll find another apartment somewhere in Jefferson."

Molly wanted to ask more questions, but the dark-haired nurse came into the room again. "Time's up," she said firmly. "Our patient needs her rest." Molly and Emily said good-bye and then headed down the stairs.

When they reached the second-floor landing,

Emily stopped and whispered, "I don't think Marta stole the sugar. Someone who was brave enough to fight the Nazis wouldn't be a thief."

"I hope you're right," said Molly. She checked to make sure that the hospital corridor was empty. "But there's someone else I'd like to visit, too."

Holding tight to the *National Geographic* she'd brought with her, Molly led the way to Room 214. The door was ajar. When Molly looked in, she saw a slim woman in a factory worker's uniform sitting next to Phillip's bed. "Oh, excuse me," said Molly.

"Come in," ordered Phillip. "This is the girl I told you about, Mom—the one who brings magazines."

Phillip's mother introduced herself as Mrs. Townsend. "It's so nice that y'all are visiting Phillip," she said, smiling and shaking hands with Molly and Emily. She was a small woman with a soft southern drawl, but her hand felt strong and calloused. "We've been so busy at work that I can't get here as early as I'd like. Today we lost almost an hour on the production line 'cause of the police, and I had to stay late to make it up."

Molly and Emily looked at each other. "The police?" Molly echoed.

"Yes," said Mrs. Townsend. She turned to her son. "You know how I told you yesterday that a pair of tires had disappeared from the warehouse? Well, today the police were questioning everybody about them." She turned back to the girls. "You know how tough it is to get tires these days!"

Molly nodded. Tires, and anything else made of rubber, were in very short supply.

"I sure hope they catch whoever took them," said Mrs. Townsend with a weary sigh. She stood up. "I need to talk with the nurse, so I'll let y'all visit together for a few minutes."

After his mother stepped out of the room, Phillip looked at Molly eagerly. "Did you bring me a *National Geographic*?"

"Yes, and it's only a month old," said

Molly, unfurling the bright yellow magazine. "And by the way, there's something I wanted to ask you. You said you've seen someone around here breaking the rules. What'd you mean by that?"

"You really want to know?" Phillip said mysteriously.

"Yes," said Molly. "It might be important. Who is it?" She paused a moment. "Is it Marta?"

"Marta?" The boy looked puzzled. "Oh, you mean the aide. Nah, not her. I'm talking about Nurse Schroeder." Phillip lowered his voice so that Molly had to lean close to hear him whisper. "She goes out and smokes cigarettes at night in the parking lot when she's supposed to be working! I know, because I can see her from here." Phillip craned his head slightly on the pillow, showing the girls how he could look out his window. "One time, Mr. Pritchard drove up in the middle of the night and almost caught her, but she ran inside as soon as she saw his truck."

"Oh," said Molly, disappointed. She didn't see how Nurse Schroeder's smoking could have anything to do with the missing sugar.

For a moment, she stared out Phillip's window onto the back parking lot below. "Do you look out the window a lot?" she asked him.

"Yeah, sure," said Phillip. "There's not much else to do, 'specially in the middle of the night. Sometimes I itch something awful inside this cast and I can't sleep. So I watch what's going on."

"Is anybody out there? Late at night?"

"You'd be surprised," Phillip said, sounding much more grown-up than he looked. "There are people coming and going all the time here—the evening nurses leave at eleven, and that aide, Marta, sometimes leaves late, too, and then there are people making deliveries." Phillip lowered his voice again. "And when old Mr. O'Grady died in the middle of the night, I saw the hearse from the funeral home that came to pick him up."

Molly glanced out the window, hoping she wouldn't see a hearse pull into the shadowy parking lot. Emily looked out the window, too, and then she turned to Phillip. "How can you tell that it's Marta who you see at night? The car park is awfully dark."

"Later on, the moon's out," said Phillip. "And Marta always parks her bicycle in the same place, so I know it's her." His eyes narrowed. "Say, why are you asking so many questions about Marta? She's not a foreign spy or something, is she?"

"Of course not!" said Emily.

"We're just testing to see how good a spy *you* are," Molly told him. "You passed!"

Phillip smiled proudly, and just then Mrs. Townsend returned to the room. Molly and Emily quickly said their good-byes and went down to the front door to wait for Mrs. McIntire.

"Isn't it strange that Marta works so late at night?" Molly asked her friend as they stood together in the entryway.

"Maybe she has a lot of work to do," said Emily.

"Maybe," Molly admitted. "But—"

Just then, they heard a door open down the hallway. Turning, they saw Mr. Pritchard come out of his office. Instinctively, Molly and Emily shrank back into the shadows of the entryway.

Mr. Pritchard didn't even look their way. He hurried along the hall in the opposite direction. As she watched the hospital director disappear down the stairs that led to the kitchen, Molly suddenly remembered something. "Phillip said that Mr. Pritchard came here in the middle of the night—in a truck!" she whispered to Emily urgently. "And didn't you say that he was driving a truck today? Was it like the one we saw at Greystone Manor?"

Emily looked down the empty hall uneasily. Then she turned to Molly. "It was closed in the back, just as that one was, and it was black," she said slowly. "But that doesn't mean very much. I saw the man from Laurence Laundry and the man from Bartle's Grocery Store in the parking lot, too. They were making deliveries, and they both had black trucks."

"But a grocer wouldn't have to steal food," Molly pointed out. "And Mr. Laurence was the one who said I should be on the lookout." Molly remembered the laundry man's warning to watch for anything suspicious. Wasn't it suspicious that Mr. Pritchard was going down to the hospital's kitchen so late at night?

"Let's see what he's doing," Molly whispered. Motioning to Emily to follow, Molly quietly walked down the hall and opened the door to the kitchen stairs. A light was burning in the hallway below, but the stairway was quiet.

"Don't go down there!" warned Emily. But Molly had already started down the stairs.

11

SUSPECTED

As she tiptoed down the stairs, Molly heard the door at the top shut behind her, closing out the light from the hallway.

Emily's not coming with me, Molly realized with a pang. For a moment Molly hesitated, wondering whether she should turn back. Then she told herself not to be a scaredy-cat.

If Mr. Pritchard is the thief, I've got to do everything I can to stop him, she decided, and she crept down the stairs.

When she reached the hall, Molly paused outside the swinging doors. She stood still and listened. She didn't hear anything, so she peeked between the doors. The kitchen looked empty.

Gathering her courage, Molly stepped inside and looked around. A single light shone above the large worktable, illuminating the large room. At the far end, starched white aprons and a chef's jacket hung neatly on pegs by the back door, as if ready to welcome the staff first thing in the morning. In the center of the room, gleaming pots were stacked by the stove. Everything was put away, and the counters were spotless. Molly began to breathe more easily. *There's nothing to be scared of in here,* she thought.

Then Molly heard footsteps coming down the hall. She looked frantically for a hiding place. The door to the pantry was open, and she ducked into it, just as the kitchen doors swung open with a creak.

Molly pressed herself against the shelves in the dimly lit pantry and listened to someone—it sounded like a man—enter the kitchen. She held her breath as the footsteps neared the pantry door. *What if it's Mr. Pritchard—and he finds me in here?* she agonized.

Then the pantry door closed with a click. Standing in the darkness, Molly heard a key turn in the lock.

She forced herself to wait until the kitchen was silent again. Then she tried the doorknob, hoping the door would open from the inside. It didn't. She pushed against the door and jiggled the knob, her hands damp with sweat.

Emily! she thought desperately. *Where are you?*

A few very long minutes later, she heard a voice from the other side of the door. "Molly? Is that you?" Emily said softly.

Molly jiggled the knob again. "Yes! I'm in here!" she called. "Let me out!"

The knob turned on the other side. But the door still didn't open. "It's locked," said Emily through the door. "How did you get in there?"

Molly briefly explained. Then she asked, "Isn't there a key around somewhere?"

After a pause, Emily said, "I don't see one."

Molly's heart fell. Then she remembered watching the chef lock the sugar inside the pantry.

"There's a chef's jacket hanging by the back door," she whispered through the door. "Maybe there's a key in the pocket."

There was another, longer pause. "I found a ring of keys," said Emily at last. "I don't know which one will fit."

Emily fumbled with the keys for a few minutes. Finally, the lock clicked and the door swung open. Molly stepped out of the pantry, feeling as if she'd been released from jail. She wiped her sweaty palms on the sleeves of her sweater. "We'd better go!" she whispered to Emily.

"Just a minute," said Emily. She locked the door again and tucked the keys back into the chef's jacket. Then the two girls ran out of the kitchen.

"Phew!" whispered Molly as they climbed the steps. "I was so scared Mr. Pritchard would find me locked in there."

"I saw him go into his office," Emily told her. "When you didn't come upstairs, I decided to look for you."

"I hope he's not around now," said Molly. She cautiously opened the door at the top of the stairs—and found herself staring into the lapels of Mr. Pritchard's dark business suit.

Mr. Pritchard stepped back, his heavy eyebrows knit together in a fierce frown. "What are you girls doing here at this time of night?" he demanded.

Emily spoke up. "You said I could come back during visiting hours to see my aunt," she said, sounding surprisingly calm. "Molly's mother brought us."

"Your aunt's room is on the third floor," he growled. "Why were you downstairs?"

Molly thought fast. "We were looking for the lavatory, sir," she said.

He scowled at her, and she looked down at the scrubbed hospital floor. As she did so, she noticed Mr. Pritchard's shoes. There was a dusting of white powder on the shiny black leather. *Where has he been?* she wondered.

"The lavatory is *not* downstairs," snapped Mr. Pritchard. "And in the future—"

But before Mr. Pritchard could finish his lecture, Mrs. McIntire called from the hospital's entryway. "Molly! Emily! Are you ready to go, girls?"

"Yes!" exclaimed Molly with a surge of relief. She and Emily darted around Mr. Pritchard and hurried out the door.

"I'm afraid my errand took longer than expected," said Mrs. McIntire as they stepped out into the cool night air. "You girls didn't have any trouble waiting, did you?"

Molly and Emily shared a glance. "No trouble at all," said Molly, crossing her fingers behind her back.

The LaSalle was parked right in front of the hospital, and it was filled with the tempting smell of fresh-baked cookies. Molly and Emily had to pile up boxes of cookies to make room for themselves on the backseat. "Gosh!" exclaimed Molly, forgetting for the moment all about Mr. Pritchard. "Did you get all these from your friend?"

Mrs. McIntire nodded. "She asked all her friends and neighbors to help bake. And, of course, we've had lots of donations at the Red Cross, too."

"Will there be enough cookies for all the soldiers?" Molly asked.

"I hope so," said her mother. Her voice sounded worried.

And I hope we can find the missing sugar, thought Molly, as she carefully balanced a plate of cookies on her lap.

Molly wanted desperately to talk to Emily about their new clues. But it wasn't until they were upstairs in Molly's room that the two girls could speak freely.

"Did you see that white powder on Mr. Pritchard's shoes?" Molly asked, sitting cross-legged on her bed.

Emily nodded. "You have something on the back of your sweater, too. Is it flour?"

Molly took off her navy blue sweater and

examined the white streaks of powder. "It looks like flour—it's probably from the pantry. And that would mean that Mr. Pritchard was in the pantry tonight, too." Molly looked up at Emily excitedly. "I bet he's the thief!"

Emily sat up very straight on her own bed, across from Molly's. "But you thought that Marta was the thief before."

"Well, yes," said Molly. She got up and threw her sweater into the laundry hamper. Then she flopped back down on her bed. "And Marta is still a possibility. But Phillip says she rides a bicycle to work. Mr. Pritchard drives a black truck. He was in the kitchen tonight, too, and I'm pretty sure he was the one who shut the pantry door."

"Do you think he knew you were in there?"

"No," said Molly. "And I'm sure glad he didn't. I wonder why he was in the kitchen so late at night."

"He could have just been locking everything up," suggested Emily.

"But he might've been stealing the sugar!" said Molly, frustrated by Emily's lack of detective spirit. "You should have come downstairs with me—maybe we could have caught him in the act!"

"It's a jolly good thing I didn't go with you," said Emily heatedly. "I was the one who rescued you, remember?"

Molly thought that calling it a "rescue" was a bit of an exaggeration, but she decided not to argue about it. She sat up and faced Emily squarely. "Look, sugar is missing from *both* the Red Cross and Oak Knoll. And my mom said that Mr. Pritchard volunteers at the Red Cross, so he could go into *both* places without being noticed. Don't you think that makes Mr. Pritchard a suspect?"

"Well," said Emily, who still looked annoyed, "Phillip's mother said that tires are missing from her factory. Do you think Mr. Pritchard goes there, too?"

"Maybe," said Molly, wondering whether Emily was deliberately trying to be difficult.

"We don't know anything about the factory's tires. Maybe they're not connected at all."

She thought for a moment and then said excitedly, "But we do know that someone with a black truck went to Greystone Manor. And we know that there are lots of bags and boxes in the cellar there. So that could be where the thief is keeping the stuff he steals. The thief would have to know that Mrs. Currier wasn't going to be home for a long time, but anyone who works at Oak Knoll would know that. Especially Mr. Pritchard."

"A cellar *would* be a good place to keep stolen supplies," Emily agreed. "It's cold and there's lots of room." She crossed her arms over her chest as if she were cold herself. "Maybe we should tell the police about Greystone Manor. They could open the cellar and look inside."

"What if the police open up the bags and find out that they're just full of old clothes or something?" Molly objected. "Ricky'd never stop laughing at us."

"You're right," Emily said with a sigh. For several minutes both girls were silent.

"But if those men we heard in the cellar *are* the thieves, we have to do something to stop them," Molly said finally. "We'll never win the war if people can get away with stealing rationed foods. I just wish we knew for sure what was in those bags." Suddenly she looked up at Emily. "Let's go back there."

Emily's eyebrows shot up. "To Greystone Manor?"

"Yes!" said Molly. "Tomorrow's Saturday, so we could go during the daytime. We'll get a good look through the cellar windows, and then we'll decide whether we should call the police or not."

Emily considered this plan for so long that Molly was sure she was thinking up arguments against it. "If we do find something, we'll tell the police, won't we?" Emily said finally. "We won't try to solve it on our own."

"Of course," agreed Molly. But in her mind she was already imagining the newspaper headline: "Molly McIntire Solves Mystery of Missing Supplies."

Won't Dad be proud of me? she thought happily.

★

In the morning, Molly and Emily ate their breakfast quickly and then took care of Bennett and Yank. As soon as the puppies were tired out from play, Molly raced into the kitchen and told her mother that she and Emily were going to ride their bikes.

"No, I'm sorry, Molly," her mother said as she washed the breakfast dishes. Mrs. McIntire explained that she would be at the Glennings Canteen all day. Mrs. Gilford would be arriving at the house in about an hour, but the housekeeper had a lot of cleaning to do, so Molly and Emily needed to watch Brad.

"All day?" asked Molly with a sinking heart. She saw her hopes for more detective work quickly disappearing.

"Until five o'clock," her mother said. "Jill will be home from the hospital by five. She'll take over then."

"Can't Ricky watch Brad?"

"Ricky has to go to his plane-spotter training," said Mrs. McIntire firmly. "Remember, Molly, we all have to work together, and I need your help today."

All our plans are ruined! thought Molly, but all she said was, "Okay."

"Some more people may drop by with cookies this morning," Mrs. McIntire continued. "So please listen for the doorbell. Mrs. Fitzgerald from the Red Cross will come by at noon to pick up any cookies that have been donated and bring them to the canteen."

"Can we take Brad to the movies in the afternoon?" asked Molly, hoping for a glimmer of fun in the day.

"All right," Mrs. McIntire agreed. "I'll leave you a dollar for your tickets, and you'll have enough left over to each get a popcorn, too."

Soon after Mrs. McIntire left for the canteen,

Jill, wearing her hospital pinafore, was picked up by a car pool. Ricky was the last to leave. *Everyone else gets to help win the war,* Molly thought as she watched her older brother bicycle down the street. *And I have to stay home with Brad!*

Half an hour later, Molly was playing catch with Brad in the backyard when she heard a voice calling over the fence. It was her neighbor, Mrs. Pederson, and she was holding a big box. "I rang at the front door and nobody answered, so I thought I'd come back here."

Whoops! thought Molly. She'd forgotten all about listening for the doorbell.

"Here are six dozen peanut butter cookies for the canteen," said Mrs. Pederson, handing Molly the box. "My son loves my peanut butter cookies. I hope the boys traveling through Glennings will like them, too."

"Thank you," said Molly, who knew that Mrs. Pederson's son was fighting in the Army. "I'll take them inside."

Molly was putting the cookies on the dining-room table when she heard the doorbell ring. It was another neighbor, Mrs. Silvano, with more cookies. And coming up behind Mrs. Silvano were two teenagers carrying armloads of cookies.

For the next three hours, Molly, Emily, and Brad did little else besides answer the door. Even elderly Mrs. Blake, who walked with a cane, arrived with a basketful of homemade lemon bars. "These are my special recipe," she told Molly, her brown eyes twinkling. "It makes me happy to know that some of our soldiers will enjoy them."

When Mrs. Fitzgerald arrived at noon, she was amazed to see cookies piled high in the dining room and the kitchen. "Your mother was right," said Mrs. Fitzgerald.

"She was?" asked Molly, puzzled.

Mrs. Fitzgerald nodded, smiling. "She was sure that people in Jefferson would come together to help our soldiers. And she was right—we're going to have more than enough cookies."

I wish I could do something to help, too, thought Molly as Mrs. Fitzgerald drove away.

Molly, Emily, and Brad ate lunch together and then walked down to the movie theater, where a cowboy double feature was playing. After the first movie, *Stagecoach,* a newsreel played. As the narrator talked about the fighting in the Pacific, Molly watched American marines battling up a hill in the face of enemy fire. She winced as guns exploded on the movie screen.

"This is scary," Brad whispered.

"Don't worry," Molly whispered back. "We're going to win this war." *We have to,* she thought to herself.

When the newsreel was over, there was an intermission, and Molly and Emily went to the lobby to buy popcorn. As they waited in line, Emily asked in a low voice, "Do you think we'll have time to go to Greystone Manor today?"

Molly hesitated. She didn't like the idea of going back to the lonely old house so late in the day, but she thought about the soldiers who had fought their way up the hill. *If they can be brave,* Molly thought, *then so can I.* "We'll leave as soon as Jill gets home," she said.

Just then, Linda and Susan joined them in line. "What are you two whispering about?" asked Susan.

"We're going back to Greystone Manor," Molly told her. "We're going to find out what's inside the cellar. Want to come with us?"

Susan and Linda looked at each other. Then they both nodded. "We want to know what's in there, too," said Linda.

★

Jill returned home at five o'clock, and a few minutes later, all four girls met outside Molly's house. They rode their bikes past Lincoln Park. Molly saw Ricky playing baseball with his friends in the park. She bicycled fast, pretending not to notice him.

The girls parked their bikes before the

steepest stretch of the hill and walked the rest of the way. At the top of the driveway, they stopped and stood silently. The late afternoon was growing cooler, and a breeze dried the sweat on Molly's face. For a few minutes, the girls watched and waited to make sure that no one was inside the house.

"It looks empty," Molly said at last. They carefully approached the house and gathered in front of the window where they had seen the bags stacked. Crowding close together, they peered in through the smudged glass. It was hard to see inside, and Molly crouched down to get a better look.

"What do you think you're doing?" a voice demanded.

12

THE LOOKOUTS

Molly jumped up and whirled around, her heart pounding wildly. Ricky and his friend David were standing several feet behind her, and they were laughing uproariously.

"Scared you!" Ricky snorted delightedly.

"Boy, did you jump!" hooted David.

"Did not!" Molly snapped.

"Did so!" said Ricky. He glanced toward Linda, who had turned around briefly and then gone back to the window. "Say, what are you doing up here, anyway? Looking for ghosts or something?"

"No!" Molly exclaimed. "And it's none of your beeswax, so—"

"It's gone!" Linda burst out.

"What's gone?" asked Ricky, elbowing his way toward the window.

"Almost all the stuff. Look!" said Linda.

Molly, Susan, and Emily crowded around the window. Peering in, Molly could see only a few sacks and boxes in the shadowy room. "Golly! Where'd it go?" Molly exclaimed.

"What's going on?" demanded David.

Susan explained that yesterday they had looked into the cellar and seen stacks of big boxes and bags of what looked like sugar or flour. "Now most of them are gone."

"Maybe you're looking in the wrong place," Ricky said. Together, the kids checked all the windows to the cellar. They didn't see the missing things anywhere.

"The thieves must've taken them somewhere," said Molly, standing up after they had looked in the last window.

Emily brushed the dirt off her knees. "'We'll be done on Saturday,'" she quoted, and then she turned to Molly. "That's what the man said, isn't it?"

"You're right!" said Molly.

Ricky scowled at his sister. "What thieves? What are you talking about?"

Molly took a deep breath and then explained how she and Emily had overheard the two men talking in the cellar of Greystone Manor. "The louder one said they'd 'be done on Saturday.'"

"So?" said Ricky. "I already told you, those guys were probably just fixing something. Repairmen always say stuff like that."

"No, you're wrong—they weren't fixing anything," Molly told him. "Mrs. Currier says she isn't worrying about repairs here anymore. She doesn't think anyone comes here at all. But Emily and I both saw the truck and we heard the men in the cellar."

Ricky was silent for a minute. "Even if they weren't repairmen," he said finally, "that doesn't mean they were thieves, either. You don't know for sure that the stuff in the cellar was stolen."

"But we do know that supplies are missing

from the Red Cross, and Oak Knoll, too," Molly argued. "And most of the things that were here yesterday are gone now."

"And today *is* Saturday," added Emily, looking worried. "The day they said they'd be done. So they may be coming back for the rest of the things today."

"Or tonight," suggested Molly, glancing at the setting sun.

Molly expected her brother to make fun of her theory, but Ricky looked serious. "Let me get this straight," he said slowly. "You think that the men you saw in that black truck are thieves. And they're coming back here sometime today to get the rest of their boxes or sacks or whatever they've got in the cellar?"

Linda and Susan both glanced over their shoulders, as if they expected to see the black truck coming down the driveway at any moment. "I'm not sure," admitted Molly. "But yeah, I think so."

"Then we'd better get out of here," said Susan.

All the kids looked at each other. Then they hurried to their bikes, and they kept riding until they reached Lincoln Park. Molly and Emily arrived last. They found the others already gathered under the oak tree on the corner.

"It'll be like plane spotting!" Ricky was saying. "Only we'll be watching for a truck instead."

"What'll be like plane spotting?" asked Molly, excited that she was finally doing something really important.

The boys explained that they were going to come back to the park after dinner. "We'll hide near the baseball diamond. If we see a black truck go up the hill, we'll follow it," said David.

"We'll watch what the guys in the truck do," Ricky added. "If they take stuff out of that cellar, we'll bike home and call the police."

Molly's heart fell. "Wait a minute. What about us?"

Ricky frowned. "What do you mean?"

"If it weren't for Emily and Linda and

Susan and me, you wouldn't even know about the black truck—or the cellar," Molly told her brother. "We're the ones who've done all the detective work, not you and David. We should be the ones to watch for the truck tonight."

Ricky laughed. "Forget it! You're too young. And besides, you're girls. Whoever heard of girl detectives?"

"What about Nancy Drew?" said Susan. "She's a girl detective."

"We mean real ones," her brother David said.

"Yeah," said Ricky. "When have you ever seen a real-life girl detective?"

Molly thought hard. With so many men away at war, women were doing all kinds of jobs in factories and offices, and even in the military. But Molly had never heard of a woman being a detective. "I don't know," she said at last, kicking the hard-packed grass with her foot. "But it isn't fair that you should get to follow the truck and not us." Molly turned to her friends for support. "Right?"

Linda shook her head. "My mom doesn't want me to bicycle after dark."

David stared at Susan. "Neither does mine," Susan admitted.

Emily looked doubtful. "I'm not sure I could ride my bike fast enough to chase a truck," she said.

"See!" said Ricky triumphantly. "You girls aren't meant to be detectives. Now come on, we'd better go home for dinner. I want to get back here as soon as I can."

It's not fair! Molly kept thinking as she pedaled furiously home. *I've got to do something—but what?*

13

THE TRAP

Jill had fixed macaroni and cheese and carrot sticks for their dinner. Ricky wolfed his down, and then he excused himself from the table. Molly sat in her chair, stabbing pieces of macaroni with her fork.

It's not fair! she thought as she heard Ricky slipping quietly out the back door.

Jill had heard the door open, too. "Where are you going, Ricky?" she called.

"Out," came a muffled reply from the back porch.

Jill got up from the table. Molly could hear her arguing with Ricky by the back door. She looked over at Emily and saw that her friend looked pale and uncomfortable. *She's not used to brothers and sisters arguing,* Molly thought.

No wonder she thinks we're strange.

A minute later, Ricky and Jill came back into the dining room. Ricky looked at Molly. "Tell Jill about the stolen supplies," he demanded. "She doesn't believe me."

Together, Molly and Emily described to Jill what they had seen and heard at Greystone Manor. "And if a black truck comes tonight, Ricky's planning to call the police," Molly concluded, looking at her brother resentfully.

"You think these people have been stealing supplies the Red Cross needed for the soldiers?" asked Jill, her eyes narrowing. "Boy, I hope they do get arrested."

"So let me go catch them!" protested Ricky, trying to get past his sister.

Jill blocked the door. "No! It's too dangerous! You and David can't go chasing criminals by yourselves."

Jill was two years older than Ricky, but he was as tall as she was. They stared at each other, face to face. "You're not the boss!" Ricky yelled.

"I am while Mom's gone!" Jill shot back.

Mom would hate to see them fighting like this, Molly thought. Suddenly she had an idea. "Wait!" she exclaimed. Both Ricky and Jill turned to her.

"Maybe we can work together," said Molly. "All of us."

Jill took a step back. "What do you mean?"

Molly began to explain her plan.

★

In less than an hour, Molly and Emily were huddled under a pine tree in the darkness near the top of Overlook Hill. They had chosen a spot just a few feet from the road. The tree hid the girls from the road, but the moon had risen and they could see the driveway leading to Greystone Manor.

Molly was keeping close watch on the driveway and listening hard for any sound of an approaching car or truck. All she heard were branches groaning in the wind.

Then there was a rustle nearby. "What's that?" whispered Emily, who wasn't used to being in the woods at night.

Molly looked up and saw a black winged creature swooping down from the sky. "Either a bat or a bird. I can't tell for sure," Molly whispered back.

She sat on the ground, her arms wrapped tightly around her knees. The wind was chilly, and she was glad that she'd worn her jacket. "Are you warm enough?" she asked Emily, who only had a sweater.

"Quite," said Emily, though she spoke through clenched teeth.

I don't think Emily would complain even if she were turning into an ice cube, thought Molly.

Molly tried not to complain either. She tried to enjoy the sweet smell of the pine needles all around her, but the needles were damp and they pricked her legs. She looked up through the pine branches and tried to count how many stars she could see. But the black night sky reminded her of how late it was, and she began to feel restless. "I wish we could play tic-tac-toe," she said.

"What's that?" asked Emily.

"You don't know how to play tic-tac-toe? It's a game where you put down X's and O's, and whoever gets a whole line of them first wins."

"Oh, you mean noughts and crosses!" said Emily. "Of course I know how to play that."

"'Noughts and crosses'!" echoed Molly. "You sure have funny words for things in England."

"English is *our* language, you know," said Emily, a bit sharply. "You Americans are the ones with the strange words."

After that, the two girls sat in silence for what seemed like forever. Molly listened intently for the crunch of gravel on the driveway, and once or twice she thought she heard it. Then the noise turned out to be only the crackling of old leaves. As the night wore on, Molly began to worry.

Maybe my plan is dumb, she thought. *Maybe we'll wait here all night and get nothing but cold and tired.*

Then another thought occurred to her. *What if the truck does come? Maybe I'll get too scared and forget what I'm supposed to do.* Molly shivered again. For reassurance, she reached up to her neck and felt the whistle she had borrowed from Susan.

I won't forget, she told herself. *And no matter what happens, I won't be a scaredy-cat.*

She tried to stretch out and realized that her right foot had fallen asleep. She was tapping her foot to wake it up when Emily suddenly put her hand out. Molly stopped and listened. There it was, the heavy sound of wheels on the narrow road.

Molly felt her heart pounding inside her chest. She stayed very still as she heard the truck come closer. Then she could see it. There were no headlights shining, but the outline of the black truck was clear against the night sky. The girls watched in frozen silence as it turned toward Greystone Manor and crackled down the drive.

As soon as the truck was out of sight, Molly jumped up. Her right foot almost collapsed under her. She stomped hard on the ground to bring her foot back to life. Pain shot up her leg, but she gritted her teeth and ran over to Emily, who was waiting for her on the road. Together, they raced down the hill.

When they reached the flat area about half-way down, Emily said breathlessly, "Is this far enough?"

Molly nodded. She pulled out Susan's whistle and blew three short blasts. Then both girls listened, straining their ears in the darkness. After a moment, three more shrill blasts sounded from the bottom of the hill.

"They heard us!" Molly exclaimed, and she and Emily ran the rest of the way down the long hill.

Linda and Susan were waiting in Lincoln Park, half hidden by the oak tree near the corner. As soon as Molly had given the signal,

Linda had passed it on to Ricky and David, who were waiting halfway between the park and the McIntires' house. It was the boys' job to ride their bikes to the McIntires' and tell Jill to call the police.

"I hope it works!" Linda declared.

What if the plan doesn't work? Molly worried as she handed the JFA whistle back to Susan. Minutes ticked by and there were no signs of the police. Molly began to pace around the oak tree. *The police have to come in time,* she thought. *They just have to!*

Then she heard gravel crunching, and she saw the black truck coming down Overlook Hill Road.

It's the thieves! she thought. *And they're getting away!*

14

CAUGHT

Wishing she could do something, anything, to stop the truck, Molly watched it rumble down the gravel road. As the truck neared the bottom of the hill, its muffled headlights came on. Now Molly could almost read the gold lettering on the side of the truck. The truck rolled closer, and she could see the words clearly: "Laurence Laundry."

Mr. Laurence lied to me! Molly realized with a sick feeling in her stomach. *He wanted me to suspect Marta—but he's the thief!*

The truck was about to turn onto the main road when a police car sped up to the intersection. It stopped close to the corner where Molly and the other kids were standing.

"They made it!" exclaimed Susan.

Ricky and David came riding up on their
bicycles. The boys had rushed back from the
McIntires' house to see what was going on at
the park. Together, all the kids watched the
policemen motion to the truck driver. The
truck pulled to a stop, and the driver opened
his door and stepped out. It was Mr. Laurence.
By the light of the patrol car's headlights,
Molly could see that he was smiling.

She felt a pang of doubt. *What if he's not a
thief after all?*

"What's the matter, Charlie?" Mr. Laurence
boomed in his loud, friendly voice. "Is there a
problem somewhere?"

Two policemen had gotten out of the patrol
car. The taller one shone his flashlight briefly
on Mr. Laurence. "Oh, it's you, Roy!" he said
with a laugh. "No, no problem. We just got
an anonymous tip about a truck with stolen
goods up on Overlook Hill. Did you see anything suspicious up there?"

Mr. Laurence shrugged. "Not a thing."
He explained that he'd been on a late-night

delivery to an estate up the hill. "You know these rich folks," he added with a laugh. "They're having a party tomorrow and they can't have stains on the maids' uniforms, can they?"

"He's lying!" Molly whispered to Ricky. "We saw the truck go right toward Greystone Manor."

Ricky nodded, his face grim. Molly watched with disbelief as the two policemen started to walk back to their patrol car together.

"We'll just drive up the hill and see if there's anything suspicious up there," the taller policeman called back to Mr. Laurence.

"Can't be too careful, can you?" said Mr. Laurence as he headed toward his truck.

"They're not going to let him get away, are they?" Linda whispered.

"NO!" said Molly.

She didn't mean it to come out as a shout, but somehow it did. The shorter policeman looked around. "What?"

"You can't just let Mr. Laurence drive away,"

said Molly, stepping forward. "Aren't you going to look in the back of his truck?"

Mr. Laurence squinted into the darkness. "What are you kids doing out at this time of night?" he demanded. He turned to the taller policeman. "Maybe these young hooligans are the ones you got a tip about."

"No! He's the one," said Ricky, stepping up beside Molly. "Look in the back of his truck."

"Yeah!" the other kids chorused, and they all stepped closer.

"Please, officer," Emily added politely.

It might have been possible for the policemen to ignore one or two kids, but they couldn't ignore six. After Emily said "Please," the shorter officer shrugged. He was a stocky, broad-shouldered young man. "Sure," he said. "Why not?"

Although Mr. Laurence protested, the shorter policeman walked to the back of the laundry truck and opened it. Molly crossed her fingers while the policeman shone his flashlight inside the truck. He gave a long, low whistle. "These sure don't look like uniforms to me," the policeman said. "Not unless they're packing them in sugar bags these days."

Mr. Laurence took off running across Lincoln Park. The stocky policeman sprinted after him and tackled him, sending him sprawling on the grassy field. The kids cheered as the policeman pulled Mr. Laurence to his feet, handcuffed him, and led him back to the patrol car. Ricky and David whistled loudly.

The taller policeman turned his flashlight on them. "Hey, you kids!" he yelled. "Get on home or you'll be in trouble!"

Oh my gosh, he's right! Molly realized. *We promised Jill we'd be home by ten!*

★

Molly, Emily, and Ricky arrived home just as Mrs. McIntire was being dropped off by her Red Cross car pool. Jill was waiting at the door. Before Mrs. McIntire could ask why they were all up so late, Jill demanded anxiously,

"Did the police get there in time?"

"Yes!" Molly, Emily, and Ricky answered together.

"And they arrested Mr. Laurence!" said Molly.

"You should have seen the tackle," Ricky chimed in enthusiastically. "That cop must've been a football player."

Mrs. McIntire looked confused. "What's this about the police? And who is Mr. Laurence?"

"He's the thief," Molly explained. "The one who's been stealing all the supplies."

"It makes sense, because he delivers laundry and uniforms to all the businesses in town," Ricky told his mother. "Including the Red Cross and the hospitals. I've seen his truck everywhere."

"And he was the person who threatened Marta, which wasn't nice of him at all," Emily added.

Mrs. McIntire sank into a kitchen chair. "Please, start at the beginning," she asked.

"Well," said Molly, sitting down beside her,

"there was a light in the cellar, only it shouldn't have been on. We wondered about it, and…"

★

After school on Tuesday, Molly and Emily biked together to Oak Knoll. Emily rode her bike easily now, and the girls made the trip in record time. Molly took her magazines to all the second-floor patients, remembering to keep two *National Geographic*s for Phillip. She saved Room 201 for last. When she finally knocked on the door, she was surprised to see her mother sitting with Mrs. Currier.

"It's so nice to see your mother again after all these years," said Mrs. Currier, beaming. "I was just telling her of some excitement I've had. The police discovered that Mr. Laurence, the laundry man, was stealing sugar, gasoline, tires, and all sorts of things to sell on the black market! He would take only a few things at a time, so most of the thefts weren't reported. Mr. Laurence's brother was helping him. And, believe it or not, they were storing their stolen goods in *my* cellar! Isn't that shocking?"

Molly tried to look surprised. "Yes, ma'am."

Molly's mother smiled. "Mrs. Currier says she wishes she had someone living in the chauffeur's apartment on her estate, someone who could watch over Greystone Manor. I told her that I thought Marta might be interested."

"She'd be an excellent choice," Mrs. Currier agreed. "Of course, I couldn't pay her much, but she'd have a comfortable place to live. And Marta is such a pleasant young woman, always willing to make me a cup of tea." She paused and looked hopefully at Molly. "By the way, dear, I don't suppose..."

"I'd be glad to get you some tea," offered Molly.

As she was leaving, Mrs. Currier called after her, "And please ask Marta to come to my room so that I can talk to her."

Molly hurried to the basement kitchen. Marta was alone in the kitchen, chopping onions on the worktable. Molly asked for a cup of tea for Mrs. Currier, and Marta nodded.

While Marta prepared the tea tray, Molly told her that Mrs. Currier would like to speak with her. "She has an extra apartment," Molly hinted. "She's looking for someone who might like to live there."

"An apartment?" asked Marta, her voice filled with excitement. Then she frowned. "I don't have much money..." she began.

"She just wants someone to watch over her house while it's empty," Molly explained, and then added, "You know that man, Mr. Laurence? He was stealing things and storing them in Mrs. Currier's cellar."

"I was told this," said Marta, nodding. "And I am not surprised. I found him once in the pantry, where he had no reason to be. I told him to go away. He tried to scare me, but I think perhaps he was scared himself."

Marta wiped her hands on her apron. "I will take Mrs. Currier her tea, yes?"

"Yes," Molly agreed, smiling. She could hardly wait to tell Emily the good news about

Marta. But just as she reached the first floor, she saw Emily walking out the back door of the building. *That's funny*, Molly thought. *She didn't even wait for me.*

Molly followed her friend out to the parking lot. Emily was standing next to her bicycle, but her back was to Molly. "Are you done already?" Molly asked her.

"Yes, I'm done," said Emily, her voice sounding slightly hoarse. Without turning around, she stretched her arm back and handed Molly a shiny new JFA whistle hanging on a lanyard. "Mr. Pritchard got us each one. He said he'd heard that we'd helped to catch the thieves, and he was very grateful. He also said he was glad that we had worked at the hospital."

"Golly!" exclaimed Molly, slipping the lanyard over her head. "That was nice. I'm sorry I ever suspected him." She admired her new whistle. Then something Emily had said struck her. "Why did he say 'had worked'? Aren't we coming back here on Thursday?"

"No," said Emily, still not turning around.

"At least, I'm not. Auntie Prim is going home tomorrow. I'm going to move into her cottage with her. So I won't have time to be a magazine delivery girl anymore."

"Oh!" said Molly. She felt as if she'd just been dunked in ice water.

Emily went on in her quiet voice. "Mr. Pritchard says it's up to you whether you want to continue here or not. I know you never really wanted to be a magazine delivery girl, so you can stop now if you'd like."

But if I stop now, Molly thought, *who will go down to the kitchen for Mrs. Currier's tea? Or remember the* National Geographics *for Phillip? And what if Mr. Emory gets another letter—who will he read it to?*

"I'll be able to give your bicycle back," Emily added. "Thank you for letting me use it."

"You're welcome," said Molly. She suddenly felt her face grow hot. *Emily doesn't care at all about saying good-bye,* she thought angrily. *She won't even turn around and look at me.*

For several long moments, both girls were

silent. "Well, I guess we'd better bike home," said Molly stiffly. Then she corrected herself. "I mean, to my house."

Emily had to turn around to get on her bicycle, and as she did, Molly saw a tear slipping down her face. "What's the matter?" Molly asked, almost in spite of herself.

"It's nothing," said Emily, shaking her head. "I'm happy Auntie Prim is better, and I'm glad she's able to go home. It's just that..." Emily hesitated. "I've enjoyed being at your house very much."

"Really?"

Emily nodded. "I always wanted to have brothers and sisters. And you've all been so kind that sometimes I've actually forgotten that I'm not a member of the family."

"Sometimes I forgot, too," Molly admitted.

Emily swallowed hard. "But Auntie Prim needs me now. She's still getting better, and I'll be able to help her with things like cooking meals. That's why I won't have time to volunteer here anymore."

CAUGHT

For a moment, Molly sat on her bicycle seat, her feet firmly planted on the ground but her mind spinning. "Why don't we both come here on Tuesdays and Thursdays?" she suggested finally. "And then afterward, I'll go to your aunt's house with you. I know how to cook hot dogs and beans, and macaroni surprise. And I can help clean up, too. If we do it together, it won't take nearly so much time."

It was Emily's turn to be surprised. She looked up at Molly, a smile spreading across her face. "You wouldn't mind?"

"It'd be fun," said Molly. "And you can keep my bicycle. We'll both need bikes so we can ride back and forth to each other's houses. Bennett and Yank will want to visit each other, too."

"That would be lovely!" exclaimed Emily. Then she grasped the handlebars of her bike and grinned. "Let's go home now—race you to the road!"

Do with less–
so they'll have
enough!
RATIONING GIVES YOU YOUR FAIR SHAR

LOOKING BACK

A PEEK INTO THE PAST

People lined up outside a butcher shop, hoping to get in before the meat is sold out

When Molly was growing up, World War
Two didn't affect just soldiers and their families—it changed everyday life for all Americans.
One of the biggest challenges was coping with
shortages of many common products, from
shoes and car tires to butter and sugar.

When America entered the war in December
1941, the United States suddenly had to produce
enough warplanes, ships, tanks, guns, and food
for hundreds of thousands of soldiers all over
the world. Many factories stopped making their

usual peacetime products so that they could help produce military supplies. In addition, the war prevented foreign goods such as coffee, sugar, and rubber from coming into the United States.

It didn't take long before everyday items grew scarce. It became hard to find boots, bicycles, bubble gum—even underpants with elastic at the waist! Grocery stores sometimes ran out of basics such as meat, toothpaste, and dish soap. Gas stations ran out of gasoline.

All of these products and many more grew scarce during the war.

To make sure that everyone got an equal share of scarce goods, the government began to *ration*, or limit, how much each family could buy.

Every man, woman, and child received ration books with numbered stamps inside that allowed them to buy a certain quantity of rationed goods.

When shoppers bought rationed goods, they had to "pay" ration stamps as well as money.

Sugar was the first product to be rationed, starting in May 1942. Soon dozens more products were rationed, too, including butter, beef, coffee, shoes, gasoline,

Cuts of meat, with their "price" in ration points

and car tires. When a family's ration stamps for a certain kind of item ran out, they couldn't legally buy any more until new stamps were issued.

Rationing forced Americans to cook differently, drive less, and make do with old shoes and clothes. Even so, most people gladly obeyed rationing laws, because they knew that rationing helped the war effort.

Some people, however, were not so patriotic. They bought or sold rationed goods illegally, or *on the black market*. The products most often purchased on the black market were the ones that people missed most— sugar, meat, tires, and gasoline.

A government poster urging homemakers to obey rationing laws

Many black-market sales involved only small quantities. A butcher, for example, might sell hamburger on the sly to a customer who had run out of ration stamps for meat. But in some cases, crooks made a lot of money. Counterfeiters sold fake ration stamps. Mobsters hijacked trucks full of rationed goods. Thieves like those in Molly's story stole items to sell on the black market.

The vast majority of Americans, however, not only took pride in coping creatively with rationing but also found many other ways to pitch in and help their country. Like Molly's family, they turned their yards into "Victory gardens" so that more canned vegetables could go to soldiers overseas. They bought government war bonds to help pay for the war. And millions of people—children and grown-ups alike—became wartime volunteers.

Kids turning a Chicago backyard into a Victory garden

The American Red Cross attracted seven million adult volunteers, who ran blood drives and cared for wounded soldiers. They also hosted *canteens,* like the fictional Glennings Canteen

in Molly's story. Homesick soldiers passing through train stations, airports, and military bases counted on the canteens for a cup of coffee, homemade food, and a friendly smile.

Soldiers at a Red Cross canteen counter

Three-quarters of all schoolchildren volunteered for Red Cross programs, too—nearly 20 million kids in 1945 alone! Like Susan and Linda, many rolled bandages and learned first aid. Teens might work in veterans' hospitals, as Jill and Dolores did.

These Junior Red Cross members packed childrens' sweaters for war refugees.

Millions of "civil defense" volunteers guarded the home front against attack. Plane spotters like Ricky, for example, scanned America's skies night and day, watching for enemy planes.

Training materials for plane spotters

World War Two was a challenging and frightening time, but it was also a time when Americans joined together to support a common cause. By doing so, children and grown-ups on the home front made a real difference in helping the United States and its allies win the war.

Children proudly collected scrap metal to be recycled into war supplies.

For Uncle Sam.... ALUMINUM! FOR NATIONAL DEFENSE From Minneapolis Kiddies

Author's Note

I don't recommend learning to ride a bike the way that Emily does in this story. I tried a similar experiment as a child and still have scars from it. But finally I learned to ride on flat ground and, like Molly, I learned to love my bicycle!

The quote that Molly reads by President Franklin Roosevelt is from his Fireside Chat on September 7, 1942. I'm grateful to the American Red Cross for the information they provided on World War Two canteens and volunteers. I'm also grateful to family and friends who told me about their experiences during the war. Molly's hometown of Jefferson, the Jefferson Red Cross, and the Glennings Canteen are all fictional, but the spirit and dedication of volunteers during World War Two were very real.

ABOUT THE AUTHOR

 Sarah Masters Buckey grew up in New Jersey, where her favorite hobbies were swimming in the summer, sledding in the winter, and reading all year round.

Ms. Buckey and her family now live in New Hampshire. She is the author of two mysteries featuring Samantha Parkington: *The Curse of Ravenscourt*, which was nominated for the 2005 Agatha Award for Best Children's/Young Adult Mystery, and *The Stolen Sapphire*.

She also wrote three American Girl History Mysteries: *The Smuggler's Treasure, Enemy in the Fort*, and *Gangsters at the Grand Atlantic*, an Agatha Award nominee.